# ABSOMOOSELY IN LOVE

*A Sunset Ridge Sweet Romance Book 7*

## JACQUELINE WINTERS

D1059939

Copy Editor: Write Girl Editing Services

Cover Design: Victorine Originals

Proofreading: FictionEdit.com

# CHAPTER ONE

CODY

Cody Evans couldn't stop a smile from forming as he stared at the two-thousand-pound moose. It was too much like the opening of a movie, something he knew more than a little about. "Gotta hand it to you, Ed. I've kayaked all over the world. Never been held hostage by a moose before." Maybe it was penance for trespassing on the late Eddie Kingsley's property.

The moose, dubbed Ed by the locals, flicked his ears forward and back as if mulling over his own internal debate. Recognizable by his unique antlers, goofy expression, and uncanny ability to inconvenience anyone who had somewhere to be, Cody knew better than to push his luck and step off the deck of the vacant log cabin. He glanced at his blue kayak, lounging on the shore, taunting him. He half thought

Mom or his sister Haylee put the beast up to this to keep Cody from leaving in two days. They were less than thrilled about his upcoming three-year absence. "You can't stop me from going."

Ed, solid as a mountain, blinked his indifference. His ears tweaked again, making Cody nervous he might be caught by travelers only the moose could hear approaching on the winding private drive. He hadn't sought permission to be here. Didn't realize he *wanted* to be here until he was more than halfway.

The kayak trip to the cabin this morning was impulsive, and one he definitely didn't have time to make. The trek back to town would take longer against the current, even for someone with his experience and endurance. But until the moose was no longer an obstacle to his way home, Cody was stuck.

Accepting he was going to be late to the annual pack-up-the-kayak-shop family breakfast, Cody leaned against a log post, folded his arms, and took in the bay view. Might as well enjoy the stolen moment of quiet. The view alone gave him an understanding as to why Eddie purchased this waterfront property years ahead of his retirement. A wave of sorrow hit Cody square in the chest when he realized his friend would never get to live out his Alaskan dream.

"Is this about the letter?"

The moose ignored the question, instead helping himself to birch leaves from the tree near the deck. In another week, two tops, the trees would be completely bare. Snow already dusted the mountain-tops; termination dust as Alaskans called it. Ed's slight shuffle to the tall birch didn't afford Cody any better opportunity to make it to his kayak unscathed.

He was still trapped on the deck.

The letter Eddie's granddaughter Jenna had given Cody last night burned a hole in his cargo pocket, but he couldn't bear to read it. *Not yet.* He was still trying to process the unwelcome news of his friend's unexpected passing. And now, there was *this*. A letter. Parting words, from one friend to another. *So, he knew it was coming?*

"Eddie, why didn't you call me?"

Cody first met Eddie Kingsley in Barbados four years earlier on a movie shoot. As a screenwriter, Eddie didn't have to be on set. But he particularly enjoyed watching the stunts. Claimed it inspired him to write.

Cody felt a lump rise in his throat. Jenna looked so much like her grandfather it nearly stopped his heart when he recognized the resemblance. Reaching to his pocket, he patted the crinkle of paper and cleared his throat. The moose looked his way, stripping another mouthful from a branch.

"If you leave now, you might make it to Mom and Dad's for breakfast," Cody said to the moose. "I know how you love fresh blueberries."

Ed's ears perked as he continued to leisurely munch, but Cody knew it was too much to hope that the creature understood even that one word. He wasn't a pet, after all. Giving up on the beast moving anytime soon, Cody dropped into a wicker rocking chair and pulled out the letter he wasn't sure he'd ever be ready to read.

He forced his eyes to the paper anyway.

*Cody,*

*If you're reading this, I kicked the bucket before I got to retire in my Alaska dream cabin. Life sucks sometimes like that. Oh well. I had a great run. My granddaughter Jenna should have hand-delivered this letter to you. I had hoped to introduce you to her, but I guess it wasn't meant to work out like that.*

*I wanted you to know it was one of my greatest pleasures meeting you. Not only are you one heck of a stuntman with superhuman talent, you're a pretty cool dude. I didn't think this old guy could learn anything new, but you taught me more than you'll ever know. You have a rare gift with the way you sense exactly what a person needs to hear.*

*Which is why I wanted Jenna to meet you.*
*I know I'm the one who owes you halibut tacos at Warren's, but I have a favor to ask of you anyway. The next page is a list of all the things I had hoped to do with Jenna when I brought her to Alaska this year. But if you're reading this, we didn't make the trip, and she's in town without me.*

*It's important to me that she gets a real feel for Sunset Ridge. I think she'll find it very inspiring if only she gives it a chance. She's got a tough exterior, which is why I know you're exactly the man for the job. I suspect she's here alone, aside from her dog. She never goes anywhere without him. Help her truly appreciate some of the experiences I had hoped to share with her before I kicked the bucket. Please. It would mean the world to this old man.*

*All my best,*
*Eddie K.*

Cody sank back into the chair, scrubbing a hand over his face. He could hear Eddie's voice in his head as he read, and grief clenched his chest tightly because of it. He remembered Eddie was supposed to visit Sunset Ridge earlier that summer, but Cody hadn't reached out when his friend didn't show. He'd written it off, deciding Eddie had a screenwriting deadline he hadn't met.

Now Cody was left with a deathbed favor he didn't have time to fulfill. His flight for Maui left out of Anchorage the day after tomorrow.

"What are you doing here?" The unexpected female voice vaulted him from the chair and to his feet. He nearly lost hold of the letter but managed to keep the wind from stealing it.

The woman with a striking resemblance to her grandfather stared back at him expectantly. Her jet-black hair, pulled back into a ponytail, danced in the breeze. The dark eyes he remembered from last night were hidden beneath sunglasses. With arms folded across her chest, Cody couldn't make out the destination screen printed across the front of her sweatshirt. "This is private property."

"I didn't mean to trespass. I was stranded by Ed—" But when he pointed toward the birch tree, he discovered the moose was no longer there. Cody turned a full circle searching for the elusive animal that had held him prisoner on the deck for over half an hour.

"Who's Ed?" Jenna Kingsley's tone was laced with suspicion, but beyond that, Cody couldn't read more. *Just like last night.*

"Local notorious moose." He leaned over the railing, as if this vantage point might suddenly bring Ed into view. He felt unsettled again that he couldn't get a good sense of Jenna. He'd traveled all over the world and met people from different cultures in every walk of life. He could read people who didn't speak a common language. *But not Jenna.*

"Grandpa said this town was small. Didn't realize that meant people named the wildlife too." She lifted one corner of her mouth slightly, reminding him of the resilient smile she'd briefly flashed him the night before at his parents' anniversary celebration. It was the striking kind of smile that left an impression, and he yearned to see it again.

"Just Ed. He's . . . special." Cody searched the acreage one last time, but there was no sign of the quirky moose. He almost mentioned how the town considered Ed a self-appointed matchmaker, but considering the letter, he didn't want Jenna to read into a comment like that. Eddie was asking him a favor as a friend, nothing more.

"You read the letter." Jenna adjusted her folded arms, her expression turning blank. If Cody could see her eyes, he might be able to get a half-decent read on her since her even tone revealed very little. He couldn't decide if she was impatient to hear what it said or annoyed that it took him so long to read it. Probably both.

"Yes, just now."

"Finally." She let out a soft sigh. "We have to stop by to tell the lawyer, and I can get—"

"Lawyer?" Cody interrupted.

Jenna removed her sunglasses, allowing them to dangle in her fingers as she studied him intently. As if debating how well she could trust him. He hadn't even had a chance to skim the list Eddie left, but he strongly suspected Jenna wouldn't be interested in completing it with him anyway. He didn't need special people-reading skills to discern that about her. "How did you know my grandpa, exactly?"

The second page of the letter itched in his palm. If he had two more minutes before Jenna arrived, he might have some idea what he was getting himself into. Now they'd have to find out together. "I crossed paths with him on a couple movie sets."

"You don't look like any actor I know."

"Never said I was an actor."

He hoped for a twinkle of curiosity to dance in

her dark eyes, but she didn't seem amused by his answer in the slightest. Eddie's comment about his granddaughter's tough exterior echoed. He understood why his friend thought Cody was the man for the job, but he already felt in over his head.

"You don't look like a screenwriting student." Jenna's assessing gaze made him feel both intrigued and vulnerable. Even more so when she slipped her sunglasses back over her eyes. "No, you like an adrenaline rush, don't you? You have to be a stuntman."

Shocked, Cody tripped on any response he attempted. People often guessed he was a beach bum or a traveler who lived out of a van. No one ever got close to the truth, and Jenna'd done it in minutes. Practically seconds. *Maybe Eddie told her about me.* "How did—" A series of barks sounded, interrupting them. "Your dog?"

"Graham. He's in the truck." Lifting her sunglasses from her eyes to her forehead, she shuffled back a couple of steps until she had a clear view of a large caramel-colored shepherd dog poking his head out the truck's half-cracked window. Eye contact seemed to calm Graham from the driveway, as he silenced instantly.

"Are you a dog whisperer?" Cody asked, only half joking.

"Look," Jenna said, setting her sunglasses on top of her head and pinning him with a serious look. "I need you to follow me to the lawyer's office so you can legally verify that I've delivered the letter to you *and* that you've read it. It was a stipulation in my grandpa's will. Please, will you do that?"

Cody suspected there was something she was leaving out, but with the unread list still gripped in his hand, he decided to circle back to that mystery later. "Don't you want to know what's in the letter?"

"I figured it was personal."

"You're not curious?"

"Sure I am." Her head dropped slightly, pointed at the folded papers still clenched in his grip. She reached out a hand. "Let me read it."

"No."

"See? Personal." Jenna let out an annoyed sigh as she stuffed both hands into the front pockets of her jeans. "Where's your vehicle?"

Cody nodded toward the blue kayak pulled onto the shore.

"Why am I not surprised?" she muttered. "Go grab it. You can put it in the back of my truck."

Folding the letter and its unskimmed to-do list, Cody stuffed it in his pocket. "It's Sunday. Mr. Jenkins isn't open today."

"Actually, he is. I called ahead in case I ran into you."

With a nod of understanding, Cody headed toward the kayak. If Ed hadn't appeared when he did, Cody would be halfway back to Sunset Ridge by now. Only a few minutes late for family breakfast instead of an hour. But without cell service, he couldn't let Mom know either way.

She wouldn't be the only one cranky about the late start today. Marc had taken the day off from the vet clinic. No doubt his older brother would have some choice words for him later. Dad, on the other hand, would just passive aggressively eat most of the leftovers. But at least Haylee, his youngest sister, would save him a raspberry crêpe.

"He doesn't bite," Jenna said about Graham as Cody walked by the barking dog and hoisted the kayak into the back of her truck. "Well, not usually."

"If I was worried about that, I'd be in the water." Cody used a loose rope to anchor the kayak in the truck bed, though with the short ride ahead, it probably wasn't necessary. But the last thing he needed was to replace it right before he left town because it'd fallen out. It'd be impossible to find a new one this time of year.

Graham sat firmly in the passenger seat, his pointed ears perked, tail wagging, and his large frame unmoving.

"Graham, you can ride in the back this once," Jenna said to the dog. He pretended to ignore her, but his twitching ear gave him away. She stared at him until he relented and looked back at his owner. "Back seat, buddy. We have a guest."

With a dramatic groan, Graham hopped over the console and positioned himself in the center of the back seat so as not to obstruct his view. Cody hardly fastened his seat belt before he felt the cold nudge of a wet nose and laughed. "Thanks for giving up shotgun, buddy." He slowly lifted his hand for inspection. After an approval lick, Cody rubbed his hand over Graham's neck.

"He likes you." Jenna's tone was flat again, making it impossible to discern whether she was intrigued or annoyed by this.

"Most dogs like me." Graham hopped to the half-opened back window as the truck started to move, freeing Cody's hand. "Cats, too."

"And moose?" The corner of Jenna's mouth lifted.

He reached into his pocket. "No, apparently not." He unfolded the letter, switching the pages immediately to keep the letter hidden. He felt certain Eddie would not want Cody to share the actual contents with his granddaughter, only the list.

"I thought you weren't going to let me read that."

"I'm not."

Cody skimmed the numbered items, surprised at how simple some of them seemed. *Breakfast at Moosecakes, watch a sunset at Lookout Point, attend a local festival—*

A series of chimes rapid-fired from his phone, causing Graham to bark twice. A litter of text messages—all from his family—filled his screen. Mom demanding to know where he was, Haylee promising to save him a crêpe, and Sadie apologizing for missing the annual family event but begging to grab dinner in Anchorage before he flew out to make up for it.

"Popular guy," Jenna remarked.

"I'm late for family breakfast."

Jenna turned to look at him, one eyebrow raised in what appeared to be genuine curiosity. "How big is your family?"

"Parents, one brother, three sisters, and one niece." Cody quickly sent a response to Haylee, hoping she'd put out the fire his absence was seemingly creating until he arrived. With any luck, they'd wait to start eating until he got there. Then he shot one off to Sadie to confirm dinner plans, secretly relieved she hadn't made the trip to Sunset Ridge this year. He loved all his sisters, but the middle one was causing an excessive amount of drama lately. "And a brother-in-law."

"Wow, that *is* a big family." She slowed for a stop sign at the end of the dirt road, waiting for an SUV to pass before she turned onto the two-lane highway toward Sunset Ridge. Cody couldn't help but scan the ditches for Ed, not that the moose's sudden presence would justify his earlier trespassing. "You all close?"

"Yeah, I'd say we are."

He wondered if his sisters would help him with the list after he left for Maui. Surely Eddie would understand if Cody couldn't personally take Jenna to do all these things—*if* she even agreed to let him.

"The thing with the lawyer should be quick," she said, a hint of apology in her voice, as they entered the city limits. Cody found it odd considering she was doing him a favor driving him back to town. He'd still be thirty minutes out at best in his kayak. "You might have to sign a form or something."

Cody held up the list, but because Graham's eager nose threatened to dampen the notebook paper, he dropped it back to his lap. "Jenna, your grandpa—"

"No." She held up her hand toward him, refusing to look over. "Let's get this over with. Then you can get to your enormous happy family."

"And what about you?"

"What about me?" She made a turn that took them down Forget Me Not Lane, but she didn't seem to notice the magnificent bay view as they snaked along it.

"Eddie never talked much about family," Cody explained. "But he did mention a couple of grand-daughters." He wished now that he'd listened closer to the stories Eddie told him, filing them away for later access. But with everyone Cody met during his travels and time on movie sets who felt the need to tell him their entire life story, it was hard to recall *every* conversation. "Is one your sister?"

Jenna stiffened, gripping the wheel at ten and two tight enough to bring out the white in her knuckles. "Whitney." She pulled into a spot outside Jenkins' Law Office and shifted the truck into park. "Let's just say I'm not upset about the lack of cell service out at the cabin." She looked back at Graham. "You stay here. We'll be right back."

Cody followed Jenna to the door, Eddie's list still clenched in his hand. "Jenna, there's something your

13

grandpa wanted me to do." He thought he had her attention when she turned back and looked at him, but the sunglasses misled him.

"This won't take long."

He wasn't the type to become easily frustrated, but Jenna was testing his impressively high patience threshold. If he wasn't heading to Maui to film a new TV series on a three-year deal, he could approach Eddie's request more delicately. But they didn't have that kind of time.

The elderly Mr. Jenkins was still tall and thin as a pencil. Seemed he'd been that way since Cody was a kid. As they entered the office, the lawyer lifted his reading glasses from his nose and set them atop his balding head. He smiled kindly at Jenna, but didn't appear to recognize her. "Hello, there," he directed to her. "Can I help—"

"I'm Eddie Kingsley's granddaughter," Jenna explained.

"Ah, yes." He waved to Jenna to follow him into his private office. "Right this way." He looked back at Cody. "You, too."

Jenna refused the chair she was offered. "I don't want to take up much of your time, Mr. Jenkins. My grandpa asked me to hand-deliver a letter to Cody Evans and to let you know when it had been read. And it has. Right, Cody?"

"Yes. But—"

"Can I have the keys to the cabin now?" Jenna asked Mr. Jenkins before he could get settled in his chair behind the desk. *Ah, the mystery is solved.* "Whatever document needs to be signed, we're happy to take care of it and be out of your hair."

Mr. Jenkins seemed taken aback. *He knows something Jenna doesn't.* Sensing he was going to be later still to breakfast, Cody silenced his phone and took a seat. Words from the list jumped out at him, but not in any coherent order. *Halibut tacos, autograph, ice cream, eagles.*

"Ms. Kingsley, I'm afraid it's not that simple."

"What do you mean?"

Mr. Jenkins looked at Cody, sympathy in his expression. "You read the letter?"

"Yes, he read the letter." Jenna didn't snap, exactly. But she was beyond feigned politeness. "I thought we already established that."

"Did you tell her?" Mr. Jenkins asked Cody, solidifying his suspicions that the local sightseeing list was not so much a suggestion but more a requirement. He'd bet those cabin keys were dependent on the thirteen numbered items.

"I kept trying to."

"Tell me what?"

Careful to separate the two sheets of paper, Cody held up the list to Jenna. "Your grandpa wants me to show you around Sunset Ridge. Said there's a few things he planned to do with you when you two came up this year . . ." He purposely let his sentence trail off unfinished for Jenna's sake.

"*Breakfast at Moosecakes*," Jenna read aloud. "*Watch*

*a sunset at Lookout Point. Spend all day at a local festival.*" She looked first at Cody, then at Mr. Jenkins. "I can do all these things without a tour guide."

"Not according to Eddie Kingsley's terms."

"There's a festival next weekend." Jenna's calm demeanor turned frantic. "I can knock all these out by then. Can't I just have the keys now?"

For the third time, Mr. Jenkins motioned for Jenna to take a seat and finally, she took the hint. "Eddie Kingsley asked that Cody Evans personally escort you to complete all the items on the list. In fact, he's requiring you provide photographic evidence for each one that includes *both* of you in the pictures."

Cody's pulse doubled as he realized what this meant. "I'm leaving town Tuesday," he said to Mr. Jenkins. "Can't one of my sisters take my place?"

"Only in the event of your death."

"That's morbid," Jenna muttered. Turning to Cody, she asked, "How long will you be gone?"

"Three years."

Hopping up out of her chair, she folded the list and tucked it into her sweatshirt pocket. "Then, I guess we better get started right away."

# CHAPTER TWO

Jenna

"There's no time for family breakfast," Jenna said to Cody outside Jenkins' Law Office. Graham's happy-go-lucky head hung out the half-opened truck window, his tall ears perked at full mast. She'd learned the hard way not to roll the window all the way down when he was younger and leapt out of the truck. It was only a miracle that she'd been parked and he landed in a giant pile of raked leaves. "There's too much on this list."

"I hate to ruin your morning, but I have obligations outside this surprise bucket list before I leave town," Cody said nonchalantly. Jenna didn't understand how he could be so calm about all this. She hadn't studied the whole list, but she suspected some items were going to be harder than others to pull off last-minute. They didn't have a moment to spare. Yet his easygoing tone lacked any sense of the urgency she felt tugging at her.

"Can't they wait until we finish the list?" Jenna realized she sounded selfish, but she was tired. Six long days on the road to get from Indiana to Alaska, including two flat tires and a shot radiator, had taken their toll on her. Not to mention the influx of texts from her pushy sister. Jenna had yet to decide what she was going to do with her grandpa's cabin. Until she got the keys and had a look inside, she wouldn't know if staying was feasible.

The last thing she could handle was being idle when such a heavy decision teetered on her shoulders.

"You can drive to my parents' place or I can walk from here," Cody suggested as casually as he might suggest having a ham and cheese sandwich for lunch. His irresistibly charming smile as he spoke irritated her. "Either way, I'm not risking the wrath of my mom by missing an annual family breakfast that rivals our Christmas morning feast."

Jenna climbed into the truck and waited until Cody fastened his seat belt to back out of her spot. She could kill an hour while he had breakfast with his family. Take Graham for a walk along the water. The pup would enjoy that after being cooped up in the truck for so many days. "Okay, we can start on the list after you're done eating. What should we do first?"

"Breakfast is only the prelude to a very busy day."

"What do you mean?" she dreaded asking.

"I have a business to close up for the winter. After we stuff ourselves full, the whole family heads to the shop to prepare everything for the chilly elements while I'm out of town."

Jenna followed his pointed finger, taking a left turn onto a residential street. "You leave town a lot?"

"Every off season."

"You said something about three years, though."

Cody rubbed Graham behind the neck, the two acting like old friends. She felt both annoyed and touched. Graham didn't warm up to just any man. He was a lover of women, but most men kept him on edge. When she offered Cody a ride earlier, she wasn't sure whether her dog would tolerate him or snap at him. But she hadn't expected the pup to practically melt at Cody's touch. "This time I'm gone a little longer."

"Why?"

"Because that's the contract I signed."

Jenna didn't want to admit her curiosity, so she feigned disinterest in the details. "How long will this winterization take?" She pulled along the curb as directed by Cody. Several cars filled the driveway of the massive log cabin. The home was nearly the size of the local lodge, where Jenna was currently staying. *This* was where his parents lived? "Couple of hours?"

He let out a laugh that annoyingly spread warmth through her chest. *So he has an attractive laugh. Get over it, Jenna. The man is leaving and won't be back anytime soon.*

"It's an all-day event," Cody explained, hand on the door handle. "We're happy if we finish up before sunset."

"What am I supposed to do all day?" she asked. "If I do any of these things on the list without you, they won't count."

He pushed open his door, giving Graham a final rub along his neck. "You could join me. If you're brave enough to meet my family. Fair warning— they're a little crazy." Cody winked at her before he shut the door, causing her heartbeat to skip and flutter.

"Join you?"

"You have something against the world's best breakfast?" he asked through the open window Jenna was waiting to roll up halfway.

"No, but—"

"Come on, then. We might get wrapped up a little sooner with an extra set of hands, you know." When she hesitated, he added, "Graham can come too, as long as you don't mind my mom slipping him bacon scraps."

Graham whined eagerly at the mention of his favorite word. Jenna *was* hungry. She'd swiped a lemon poppyseed muffin from the lodge earlier, but her rumbling stomach reminded her that it'd been hours ago. "Fine, okay. But the second we're done, we knock out everything on this list we can tonight. Deal?"

"Deal." Cody clapped the truck door with his hand. "Now, hurry up before my dad eats all the cheesy hashbrown casserole."

Jenna wiped sweaty palms against her jeans as she followed Cody inside, Graham happily trotting at her side on a leash. She could hear the dull roar and occasional burst of laughter from an open window. His family sounded . . . blissfully normal. Like the large kind of family she'd often dreamed she was really a part of.

Except, since a young age, Jenna only had her grandpa and older sister.

Now it was only Whitney.

"Sorry I'm late," Cody announced as they stepped into the dining room. The large table seated eight—nine if you counted the baby girl in a highchair. Six of the chairs were filled. A massive spread of waffles, crepes, bacon, sausage links, a couple of casseroles, and fresh fruit covered the table. "I brought us some help."

The room fell silent as several sets of eyes zeroed in on Jenna, making her wish she could disappear. She hated attention from strangers in situations such as these. What on earth had she been thinking by accepting Cody's invitation? It wasn't too late to shuffle backward and slip out the door. She could find *something* to do to kill time until this evening.

"I'll grab another plate," the young woman seated next to the highchair said. Her dark chocolate hair was pulled into a messy bun and her eyes sparkled with curiosity. Jenna guessed the girl was still in high school. "Cody didn't tell us he was bringing a *friend*."

"Jenna's the granddaughter of a dear friend of mine," Cody explained, guiding her to an empty chair. "And this is her dog, Graham. Since we have an empty chair, I invited them to join us."

"Eddie Kingsley," the eldest woman in the room said, recognition in her tone. Jenna guessed the woman with chin-length silvering blonde hair was Cody's mother. Her soft smile radiated warmth, helping calm Jenna's frayed nerves as she slipped into a chair. "You're the spitting image."

"You knew my grandfather?"

"Knew?" She looked to Cody, her expression falling.

"Eddie passed away earlier this summer." He gently patted Jenna's shoulder as he took the seat next to her. The gesture meant to provide comfort made her pulse quicken. She refused to dwell on why. "Jenna has a few things her grandpa wanted her to do in Alaska. Touristy things. Once we've got the shop packed up, I'm going to help her."

"I'm so sorry for your loss, dear." Cody's mother offered her a sympathetic smile, forcing Jenna to focus on an arrangement of flowers in the center of the table. She'd cried enough the first few weeks after Grandpa passed. She was *not* about to open the floodgates all over again in front of strangers.

"Thank you," she managed to say without her voice cracking.

"Now that Cody's here, can we eat? We're already behind schedule."

"That's my brother, Marc," Cody explained, leaning closer to Jenna. Another inch or two and their shoulders would brush. *Flowers. Focus on the flowers.* "Wears a permanent frown and is up in the running for world's grumpiest man. Ignore him."

"Please, dig in," Cody's mother announced.

As bowls and serving plates passed around the table, Cody gave entertaining introductions of his large family in between their excited chatter.

His mother, Beth—the best cook in southeast Alaska and bravest woman in town for birthing *five* Evans siblings—sat directly across from Jenna. "We can't convince her to enter the baking contest at the Blueberry festival to prove her natural talents, but Cody's not wrong," a blonde woman agreed. "She's an amazing cook."

"That's Laurel and her husband, Chase. She's the only sister who's older than me. Those two have quite the story, but you'll have to ask them to tell it." Cody moved around the table, rapid-fire style. "There's my dad, Jerry—hardest working man I've ever met, and I've met a *lot* of people. He can put away an entire nine-by-thirteen pan of cheesy hashbrown casserole, which should be motive enough never to be late to breakfast again, should you find occasion to join us in the future."

Laughter echoed around the table, making Jenna wish she was more than a misfit guest. She'd only known the Evans clan for ten minutes, and yet she already knew she loved them.

"Last but not least at the table, there's my youngest sister, Haylee and her daughter—the cutest niece in the universe and future heartbreaker—Melly." Jenna kept her surprise to herself, locking in her expression. Haylee didn't look old enough to *have* a child as she appeared to be one herself. The little girl in the highchair looked six to eight months old, if Jenna had to guess.

"You forgot to mention that I'm the *best* sister," Haylee said, flashing a cheesy grin that made Melly giggle.

Jenna looked at Cody. "I thought you said you had three sisters?"

"Sadie doesn't like getting her hands dirty," Haylee answered with an eyeroll. "Or, you know, working in general."

Cody bit down on his bottom lip, but only briefly enough for Jenna to notice. *He knows something he can't share.* "That's not entirely fair," he said, his tone completely calm. "Sadie works very hard—in *Anchorage*. It's a little bit of a drive, and she doesn't always make these family events."

"Cody's being nice," Haylee chimed in.

"Haylee," Jerry said in warning.

24

"What?" Haylee asked, feigning innocence. "*Mom* won the bet."

"Really, Mom?"

Beth dabbed her lips with her napkin. "I know my own daughter. It's not my fault I won twenty bucks because I expected her to cancel fifteen minutes before she was supposed to show up." Beth looked at Jenna. "For the record, she called *fourteen* minutes before."

Cody let out a soft groan that was nearly inaudible, but it and Beth's comment made Jenna silently chuckle. Had her smallish family *ever* felt this much . . . fun? She tried to remember a time from when her mom was still alive that carried the same warmth as this moment did now, but she couldn't find one.

"And that's the gang." In a quieter tone, Cody said to Jenna, "Can you guess why I go away for the winter?"

Jenna thought if she had a family this big and wonderful, she'd never leave. Growing up, her grandpa was often gone for weeks at a time on one movie set or another. He wasn't required or even expected to show up for filming, but his clout in the industry and desire to be where the action was born earned him a reserved seat whenever he requested one.

Since the age of nine, that left Jenna alone with her older sister, Whitney. She loved her because Whitney was family, and you were supposed to love family. Even when they drove you up a wall and constantly belittled every mistake you made.

Jenna barely cut her waffle in half before Beth directed a question at her. "How long are you in Alaska, dear?" The woman's sweet tone made Jenna's heart squeeze. Having lost her own mother when she was only nine left a big hole in her heart she wasn't certain would ever be filled in this lifetime. Whitney had certainly never *tried* to fill it.

"I'm not sure," Jenna answered truthfully. "At least a week. Could be longer, though." Unbeknownst to anyone back home, Jenna had towed all her belongings in a covered trailer in case she chose to stay. The cabin would be hers to do with as she pleased once this bucket list nonsense was finished. But moving to Alaska was a big decision, one she wouldn't make lightly.

The only thing she did know for sure was that she wasn't going back to Indiana. Grandpa's death made one thing *very* clear to Jenna. It was time to sever the cord with her toxic, controlling sister. She could love Whitney from afar, and that would have to be enough for both of them.

"Too bad Cody's leaving in two days," Haylee said, a heavy emphasis on the word *two*. "Maybe he should stick around a few more so he can show you around. Most of the tourists are gone for the season, so it's the perfect time."

Jenna glanced at Cody, more curious than she wanted to admit about his reaction. She couldn't recall Grandpa mentioning a stuntman who lived in Alaska. Yet she felt a connection to Cody she couldn't explain. One that might only exist *because* of her grandpa. Didn't matter that she didn't know him or that she'd caught him trespassing only an hour earlier. She wanted him to stay, too. None of it made sense.

"I'm not here to inconvenience anyone," Jenna said after a chatter erupted about Cody's departure date. "Cody's already graciously agreed to help me with my grandpa's list before he leaves." She left out the part about the cabin being tied to the completion of that list. She should've known Grandpa would attach strings to her inheritance. She could hear his voice in her head saying *It's for your own good, Jenna.*

"Nonsense," Beth said, discreetly slipping Graham a strip of bacon under the table. Jenna knew because she felt the excited swish of her dog's tail against her leg. "I remember your grandpa. He was a kind, generous man. We're happy to have you for breakfast —or any other meal you want—while you're in town."

The conversation thankfully fell away from Jenna's life and transitioned to theirs. She pretended not to eavesdrop, but she was silently fascinated with the Evans family. How many times had she dreamed of being part of a large, loving family with siblings who might bicker and tease, but showed no doubt that they loved each other? And *both* parents in the picture, still happily married.

"There's still time to escape," Cody said, his voice

low. He was teasing, but he was also giving her an out if she wanted one.

Jenna stroked Graham's neck as she contemplated her options. Now that the dog had been sated with bacon—and there was none left to beg for anyway— he rested his head in her lap. He was a ball of energy, but he tired after a burst and took long naps. Snoozes that were great for Jenna's creativity. She'd written and illustrated dozens of children's books with Graham Cracker curled up at her feet.

Until Grandpa Eddie died.

"I don't have anything better to do," Jenna finally said. Maybe spending the day with the Evans family would inspire the new children's book series her agent and editor were both not-so-patiently request- ing. They'd been understanding all summer while she mourned, but time was against her now. And Jenna didn't even have a loose idea to pitch, much less a sample to send.

"I want it on the record that I gave you an oppor- tunity to escape," Cody said over the rim of his cup of orange juice.

Jenna watched as Laurel and Beth cleared the table, both refusing her offer to help. Melly fussed as Haylee wiped her mouth with a wet cloth like a pro. The men were huddled in conversation about a base- ball game. Marc had yet to smile *once* this entire breakfast, even with both Jerry and Chase talking excitedly about some big play.

"I like your family."

Cody lifted a corner of his mouth in a lopsided smile that made a butterfly or two flutter in her stomach. "It's not just spending the day with the Evans clan. It's hard work."

Realizing that she had yet to ask what type of business they were packing up for the winter, she wondered what she agreed to. But Jenna wasn't one to go back on her word. She agreed to help, and help she would. "What is this business anyway?"

"Evans Kayaking Adventures and Rentals."

Jenna laughed so suddenly she nearly spit water at Cody. "How did I not guess that?"

"I do have a car, for the record. But I wanted to take a kayak out once more before they were all cleaned and packed up."

"For the next three years?"

Cody shook his head. "It'll open next season, like it always does. I just won't be home to manage it in person."

"Because you'll be where?"

"Maui," Haylee answered for him. "Don't feel sorry for him. We don't."

Jenna decided she was too curious to act as though she didn't care. "What's in Maui?"

"There's a new—"

"C'mon, you two," Marc said, wearing the same frown from earlier. She'd thought Cody was exaggerating, but now she wasn't so sure. He did seem permanently brooding. Some women might find that whole persona attractive. She much preferred a man who wasn't afraid to smile. "Sooner we get started, the sooner we're done."

"Jenna," Haylee said as she scooped Melly into her arms. "I hope you don't regret offering to help. I really like you. It'd be a shame if we scared you off."

# CHAPTER THREE

Cody

Cody hammered in the last nail on the two-by-four across the shed door, earning a round of cheering from his family and Jenna. Graham and Zeus, Laurel and Chase's dog, both let out a series of barks when he finished, caught up in everyone else's excitement. The long day of cleaning kayaks, checking gear, taking inventory, and packing everything away for winter was finally over.

"And that's a wrap," Marc announced, his light-hearted tone betraying his brooding expression. "Can we go home now?"

"I need a picture first," Mom hollered, grabbing Marc by the arm. "It's tradition."

Cody stood with his back to the nailed-up shed doors as his siblings and dad gathered in around him.

"Jenna, you too," he called when she slipped off to the sidelines.

She shook her head, glancing at Cody. "I'm good." Though spending the day working beside her hadn't made Jenna any easier to read, he thought he saw through her in this particular moment. She yearned to be in the family photograph but didn't think she deserved to be. It made him all that more curious about her home life and background. People fascinated Cody on a basic level, but this was something more.

"Jenna, you should be in the picture," Mom insisted. "You earned it, young lady."

"What about you?" Jenna asked.

"I earned the right *not* to be in the picture." Mom gently nudged at Jenna's shoulder. "Go on, sweetie. There's no dinner until I get my annual photo, and the boys will get growly until they're fed."

Cody reached out an arm for Jenna, allowing her to slip into the back row. She was shorter than him, but taller than Haylee by six inches. He left his hand on her shoulder while Mom made them count to three multiple times, fully expecting Jenna to shrug it away. She'd been amazing today. Not only was she not afraid to lend a hand and do whatever was asked of her, she fit in as if she'd always been a part of the Evans clan. His family fell in love with her instantly, and Cody didn't know what to make of that.

They weren't even friends. Merely acquaintances brought together by a common death.

"Are we done now?" Marc growled.

"Yes, we're done."

Jenna spun, facing Cody. "We still have time to do a couple things on the list tonight, right?" Her guard was definitely down from this morning, but her determination reminded him she saw him as a means to an end. *Nothing more.*

"If we go now, we can catch the sunset at Lookout Point." Cody hadn't seen the list since Jenna stuffed it in her sweatshirt pocket that morning. Until he had a chance to look it over, he wasn't certain what he was in for. Or if it was possible to complete all thirteen items before he left town.

"That sounds like somewhere high schoolers go to make out," Jenna said, her eyebrows raised in suspicion. "Grandpa really wanted to take me there?"

Cody let out an easy laugh, enjoying her expression far too much. "I promise, it's not what it sounds like. It's actually the best spot in all of Sunset Ridge to watch the sunset. You get a little bit of everything from that vantage point—trees, mountains, ocean. It's a view you have to see to really appreciate."

"They could pick a better name," she surmised as she led them to her truck. Cody offered to drive them earlier, but she was insistent that Graham liked his own truck and would make a fuss if stuffed into a car. At least the dog was allowing Cody to ride shotgun. "Which way do I go?"

"Head to the lodge."

"Really?"

"The trail starts behind the lodge. Did they not mention this place to you when you checked in? It's only a short hike away."

"Hike?" Jenna slowed for a stop sign, waiting for an oncoming car to pass. When the passenger—Tillie Grant—waved at them, Jenna looked confused. Cody waved back to Tillie. "You wave to everyone here or is she part of your massive family, too?"

"You're from the Midwest. You don't wave at everyone?"

"Not where I'm from." She rolled through the intersection, the lodge coming into view a block later. The massive log structure sat atop a hill, the setting sun reflecting off the logs and making them glow that rich cedar color. "We really have to hike?"

"You should be happy about this," Cody said as she pulled into a gravel parking spot. "If you could drive to the spot, teenagers *would* be making out up there."

Thankfully, the winding trail only required them to travel a couple hundred yards to the lookout point. Graham zigzagged on his leash the whole way, apparently still high on energy from the exciting day and making a new four-legged friend.

With the sun setting so rapidly, they barely made it. But Cody didn't have time on his side. With a rainy day in the forecast tomorrow, there likely wouldn't *be* a sunset to watch then.

"This is it?" Jenna looked around as a yawn escaped, sounding unimpressed. Possibly even disappointed. Graham, on the other hand, found all the new smells *very* pleasing. Cody tried not to laugh at the duo both facing the wrong direction, completely missing the mountain and ocean view.

He cupped Jenna's shoulders and gently turned her toward the water view. "*This* is it."

It didn't matter that Cody had traveled all over the world and watched sunrises and sunsets alike in several different countries. Lookout Point at sunset—right here at home—stole his breath away every time. The view offered everything—snowcapped mountains, houses scattered amidst the trees, and pristine water reflecting the oranges, reds, and pinks of the sky. A sunset in Maui might rival this view, but it'd never surpass it in Cody's opinion.

"We need a picture," Jenna said flatly, pulling him out of the breathtaking moment. She retrieved her phone from her jeans pocket and lifted it in front of her. After a few angle adjustments, she instructed, "Get closer."

"Here," Cody said, taking the phone from her soft fingers. "I can reach farther." He tried not to let her lack of reaction dampen his spirits as they brushed shoulders and smiled for the camera. Eddie had asked him to escort Jenna *because* of this, he reminded himself. Because she needed someone to help her leave behind the checklist and enjoy the moment.

After snapping a couple of photos, he returned to watch the sunset, leaning on the split-rail fence. Graham groaned, dropping at his feet. After a hard day's work, Cody was starving. But he wasn't going to waste the last few minutes of an amazing sunset. It'd be three years before he'd see it again. *Maybe longer*. If anything, he should be thanking Eddie for this moment he wouldn't otherwise have found the time to experience and tuck into his memories.

"What's next?"

Cody swallowed a groan. He certainly had his work cut out for him. "You're missing the sunset, Jenna."

"I saw it."

Refusing to move from his perch until the last of the colorful array disappeared from the sky, Cody asked, "Did you know your grandpa loved sunsets?"

"I know."

"Did you ever watch them with him?"

"I used to. When I was little." She let out a sigh, but relented and joined him at the fence. She leaned against it and peered west. The colors were fading now that the last sliver of the sun slipped below the horizon. "He used to tell me the colors were painted across the sky with a giant, invisible paintbrush."

If Cody wasn't mistaken, a hint of a smile appeared across Jenna's lips. With her standing nearby, he could scoot a couple inches closer, lean down—he shook away the irrational thought before it had time to take root. Cody didn't get involved with women locally. He dated occasionally on his travels, but he accepted long ago that he'd never settle down. Someone local would expect that of him.

And Jenna . . . it wouldn't be fair to lead her on. Eddie would surely haunt him for that.

"You know, it's actually the reason I started painting with watercolors. Somewhere there's a box with hundreds of watercolor sunset pictures. I was only four when that craze began, so naturally it's my best work."

"Naturally." Cody was so shocked by the rare unguarded moment she shared with him, he didn't want to spoil it by so much as breathing.

"Okay, I see why this made the list," Jenna added, swiping at the corner of her eye with a knuckle.

He yearned to ask her so many questions. Questions whose answers would be so much easier to draw out of anyone else. But prying, no matter how gentle or suavely, would only cause her to close up. That much he now understood about Jenna Kingsley.

As the final hints of red and orange faded, giving way to a dusky blue that blended with the water, Cody pushed up from his perch on the fence. He took a quick scan of the area known for occasional black bear visitors. "I remember something on that list about ice cream," he said once he confirmed they were alone.

"Yeah. Something about a moose something ice cream sandwich."

"Ah, that'll be a moose tracks ice cream sandwich from Glacier Ice Creamery." He glanced at his watch, uncertain whether the local ice cream parlor had switched yet from summer tourist hours to their off-season hours. Most places in town were switching next week, but some had already made the change. "We better head that way. If they're still open, they'll be closing up shop soon."

Graham hopped to his feet, his wagging tail suggesting he was ready for another adventure. But his sleepy eyes begged for bedtime.

They rode downtown in silence, only the back driver's window rolled halfway down. The days were still unseasonably warm, but the chilly evenings made up for it. Jenna flipped on the heater for the short trek.

She left Graham in the truck with a promise to bring him back a *pup cup* if they had one.

All the lights were still illuminated, allowing Cody to feel the slightest relief. He remembered several food items on the list and didn't feel up to eating them *all* in one day. "After you," he said to Jenna, holding the door open.

Not only were they the last two customers of the day, they snagged the last two moose track ice cream sandwiches. Jenna asked the teenage girl behind the counter to take their picture before they found a booth. Ice cream was not his typical dinner, but tonight it'd have to do. He felt exhausted and ready to call it a night, but they needed a game plan for tomorrow if they had a prayer of knocking out the remaining eleven things before he left for Anchorage.

"These are great!" Jenna flashed Cody one of her rare, dazzling smiles. It was the kind of smile that could stop traffic at rush hour and make men forget their own names. "They're *shaped* like moose heads." She nibbled at an antler, moaning in delight at the flavor. Her eyes fell closed as she savored the dessert.

"They make their own ice cream," Cody explained, relieved he didn't have to convince her to slow down and enjoy this particular moment. Maybe she wouldn't make every sightseeing task so difficult after all. "Including these moose-shaped cookies."

"Fun fact about me," she said between bites, "I *love* ice cream. It's like my kryptonite. Grandpa knew it, too." Her smile fell slightly. "I wonder what he was buttering me up to tell me. He always used ice cream to catch me off guard."

Cody had a couple of theories, but he suspected Jenna was already considering them. No need to dampen the mood with such morbid thoughts. Instead, he shifted gears. "Where's the list? We should probably make a plan. I still haven't packed, and there's a few people I need to say goodbye to."

Unfolding the list, Jenna placed it on the table between them. "First one—breakfast at Moosecakes." She looked up at him. "What's a *moose*cake?"

"You'll find out tomorrow morning. We can start our day there."

"We did number two: watch the sunset at Lookout Point." She slipped out of the booth, borrowing a pen from beside the register. She ran a purple ink line through the second item, then skipped down to the thirteenth one they were completing now and did the same. "Number three: attend a local festival and spend all day there." She looked up at Cody. "I don't suppose there're any surprise festivals tomorrow?"

"No." Cody scrubbed a hand over his face. The next festival was this coming weekend. The same weekend he was supposed to spend getting settled into his new place in Maui. Filming began the Monday after. "Let's circle back to that one."

"Moving on. Number four: dance under the northern lights." She looked at him, then out the window. "Don't suppose—"

"They might come out later, if the clouds clear." Which, based on tomorrow's overcast, rainy forecast, was unlikely. Surely there was some sort of clause for circumstances outside of their control? He'd have to have a chat with Mr. Jenkins and find out what loopholes—if any—he knew about.

"Number five: meet local moose legend, Ed." Jenna looked up at Cody, her expression a mixture of amusement and disbelief. "You're kidding me. He's *real?*"

"Yes, he's real."

"I thought you made that up so I wouldn't get mad at you for trespassing."

"Ask anyone. Ask Aria." He pointed to the teenager behind the counter. "Aria, do you know who Ed is?"

"The moose? He's practically a celebrity around here."

Jenna shook her head, unable to keep in her laughter as she struggled to finish the last of her sandwich. "No wonder my grandpa loved this place. Makes me wonder if he wrote any movie scripts featuring a famous local moose."

Cody slid the list closer to him, reading off the next item. "Halibut tacos at Warren's Sea Shack. Of course, Eddie." When Jenna looked at him curiously, he explained, "Your grandpa owes *me* halibut tacos. I helped him haul a heavy desk up to the loft of that cabin. He thought the ocean view from up there would inspire him."

"You've been inside the cabin?" Jenna's smile faded as emotion filled her eyes.

"Yeah. Couple of times. You'll love it." The urge to slide out of his booth and into hers so he could drape an arm over her shoulders tugged at him with startling intensity. But Cody kept himself rooted to his spot, uncertain how Jenna might react. They were practically strangers who'd only spent one day together. That didn't qualify him to go around offering her hugs.

"I've only been able to peek in the windows," she admitted, spinning the list on the table with her index fingers and refusing to look up at him. "With all those heavy drapes, I can't see much."

"Blackout curtains."

"Yeah, I guess."

"Some people use them in the summer when it doesn't get that dark." Cody stopped the list from spinning and read the next item. "Seven: watch Jenna read one of her picture books at the local children's story hour." He looked up in surprise. "You're an author?"

Jenna seemed unsettled by the item, yanking the list away from Cody to read the words for herself. "I'm not doing this one," she muttered. "Grandpa knows I don't—*knew*." She squeezed her eyes shut, inhaling deeply. "I'll talk to Jenkins in the morning. I can't do this one."

"Are you published?" Cody asked, genuinely curious.

"Yes." Jenna let out her deep breath. "Moving on. Number eight says we need to spot more than eight eagles in one day."

With each added item, Cody felt the truth seeping in. There was no way they could complete this list before he left town. *Unless I change my flight.* "Eagles are the only birds who don't let the rain stop them from hunting prey," he explained. "But they do hover above the rain clouds making it pretty hard to see them flying around."

"And this matters because?"

"Because it's supposed to rain all day tomorrow. Doubtful we'll see any."

Cody wondered how upset his booking agent would be if he told Holden he'd be late getting to Maui. The deposit on the beachfront home was already paid in full. The property management company wouldn't care if he came a couple days later than planned. The check for the first month's rent would be for the same amount. He'd miss out on a stunt crew dinner, but he could introduce himself on his own.

"Guessing tomorrow would be a pretty crappy day to go—" She held the list closer to her eyes. "Bear Glacier kayaking?"

"Yeah, that's a day-long activity by itself." Cody already knew the truth, but it was impossible to deny any longer. He didn't have a choice but to push out his flight to Maui. The contract didn't require him to be there until next Monday morning. He'd be pushing things close, but he couldn't leave Jenna with a half-finished list and no cabin.

"What do we do, then?" She looked at him apologetically, though it wasn't her fault Eddie put them in this predicament. "I don't have anywhere to—" She cleared her throat. "Cody, I can't wait three years for this cabin."

Tomorrow, he'd call Holden and get his schedule adjusted. The chewing out that came with rearranging plans last-minute was a necessary evil in order for him to do the right thing. "Don't worry." He covered Jenna's hand with his own so briefly the zing of electricity at the contact *almost* didn't affect him. "I'll stick around town a few more days. We'll get the list done before I leave."

# CHAPTER FOUR

Jenna

A string of rapid-fire pings caused Jenna to jolt up in her bed. Her phone lit up in the dark room, vibrating its way dangerously close to the edge of the night-stand. She snatched the pesky device half a second before it was destined to crash to the floor.

From the edge of the bed, Graham groaned his displeasure at being disturbed so early.

"Believe me, buddy. I wouldn't be sad if it broke, either." She dragged her index finger along the screen, unsurprised that Whitney's name was attached to every notification except one. The girls in the office had yet to remove her from the group text about a last-minute happy hour tonight. They would shortly after Jenna sent in her two-week notice and word got around that she wasn't coming back from this vacation.

Jenna flipped on the light, and Graham groaned again.

"My grumpy old man dog," she teased, rubbing his belly when he rolled onto his back and lifted all fours in the air.

She wasn't ready to skim her older sister's texts. No doubt it was about the wedding. Never mind that Jenna had made it clear she wasn't attending. Or maybe Whitney was crabbing about the state that Jenna left the basement when she moved out all her belongings. Jenna purposefully forgot to vacuum her former bedroom and didn't wipe out the bathroom sink. She knew what gripes her sister would have.

"We better get you outside, Graham Cracker."

She traded her pajama bottoms for jeans and slipped on a jacket. Only when she reached the lodge's back door did she wish she'd grabbed the waterproof one. Cody was right about the rainy day. At the thought of seeing him again, she started to smile. But she caught herself in time to keep it from fully forming. *He's not staying. No point in getting involved beyond the list.*

As the morning sun began to illuminate the horizon, rain fell in steady sheets; not heavy but definitely more than a drizzle.

"Let's make this quick, okay?" They raced out the door together, and Graham made quick work of things. For a dog who loved to jump in a lake and swim until he was ready to pass out, he hated getting rained on.

When they made it back to the room, Jenna's phone was ringing. The temptation to chuck it into the ocean had never been stronger. "At least when we move into the cabin, no one will be able to reach us on this thing." She considered ignoring her phone, but with the three missed calls right before it, Whitney would just call back again and again until she answered.

"Hello?"

"*There* you are." Whitney's tone was as condescending as Jenna expected. Unlike the Evans clan, there was little to no actual love between her and her sister underneath the bickering. It made her yearn for Beth and Jerry to adopt her. "Is your phone broken or something?"

"No." Jenna learned long ago that explanations were considered excuses, and Whitney was always eager to pick those apart.

"Then why didn't you answer?"

Graham stood at the door, reminding Jenna she'd yet to towel-dry him off. The only thing he tolerated about the rain was the rub-down afterward. She grabbed a towel from the bathroom, smiling as he popped onto all fours and eagerly wagged his tail. "Did you need something?"

"Yes! Didn't you read my texts?"

"Not yet."

"Why not?"

"Whitney, I don't have time for the fifth degree. Whatever it is, spit it out. I won't have much cell service the rest of the day." Most of the items Cody suggested they complete today were local, but that didn't mean Jenna needed to carry her phone. Or even leave it turned on back in the lodge room.

"You haven't ordered your bridesmaid dress." Whitney's overexaggerated tone made Jenna roll her eyes. "Did you even get measured for it yet? I know we talked about you losing five pounds first—"

Jenna tensed, unsurprised that her sister would ever actually *listen* to a thing she said. "I already told you, I'm not coming to the wedding."

"Of course you are. Without you, we have an uneven number. You know I can't stand odd numbers." Typical Whitney, convinced she controlled the universe. Jenna wondered what kind of meltdown her older sister would have if she found out Jenna hadn't put the trailer of her belongings in storage as they discussed, but drove it up to Alaska instead. The thought brought her a slice of malicious joy. "Now, if you put on some extra pounds that's okay. Just tell her—"

Another call beeped through, and Jenna pulled her ear away. An odd flutter danced in her belly at Cody's name on the screen. "I have to go. Grandpa gave me lots to do."

"He's gone, Jenna. This trip of yours . . . it's not healthy."

"Gotta go, bye." She ended the call so she could

answer Cody's, refusing to let her emotions trigger from Whitney's crappy and misguided comment.

"Did I wake you?" he asked, that suave honey-smooth voice filling her with warmth. Jenna couldn't explain why she was having such a strong reaction to a man she'd known only one day. It didn't help that he was kind, funny, and attracted people to him like a magnet. Or that he was incredibly easy on the eyes with his tall muscular frame and sea-green eyes that put anyone who dared to gaze into them in a trance.

"No, that honor belongs to my overbearing sister."

"Well, in that case, you want to knock number one off the list and meet at Moosecakes for break-fast? I'd offer to pick you up, but I don't want to get on Graham's bad side."

*This* was exactly what was luring Jenna in. Cody's charismatic charm and the way he was about her fur-child. "I thought I might leave Graham to nap in the room while we grabbed a bite. He'll just mope in the truck with all this rain."

"I'll pick you up in ten."

"No, that's okay. I'll meet you there."

Jenna ended the call before Cody could object and immediately leapt from the bed. She was still half in pajamas, her hair was a bird's nest trapped in a ponytail, and mascara smudged beneath her eyes. She wasn't trying to *impress* Cody. That would be ridicu-lous. But considering there would be photos, she did want to look semi-presentable.

Graham groaned, stretching out on the bed.

She fished a treat from the backpack she'd stuffed full of his goodies before they started this road trip, and promised to be back soon. He'd made it two nights now without munching on a pillow—a nervous trait from his puppy days when he feared she would leave and never come back.

"Good morning," one of the staff greeted cheerfully as Jenna came down the hallway. The woman with dark chocolate-colored hair pulled back into a high ponytail looked vaguely familiar, though Jenna didn't recall having seen her at the lodge since she checked in. "I'm just finishing up a pan of white chocolate raspberry muffins if you're hungry."

"That's the wonderful aroma I smell."

The woman wiped out a display case with a damp rag. Jenna recalled seeing it empty except for crumbs when she made it back to the lodge the night before. "It's a new recipe I've been dying to try," the woman explained. "Shouldn't be more than ten minutes."

"Actually, I'm headed to some place called Moose-cakes." Jenna debated how much to share with the woman, who despite her unexplainable familiarity, was still a complete stranger. "I'm supposed to meet a friend."

"How about I save you one?"

Jenna felt a layer of ice around the outside of her heart crack and fall away. There were still several layers fortified in place, but in only two days, the town of Sunset Ridge was embracing her in a way she'd never experienced at home. She was beginning to understand why her grandpa planned to retire here. "That would be wonderful, thank you."

"What room are you in?"

"Seven. But my dog's in there. He'd help himself for sure."

"Dog person. I knew there was a reason I liked you." The woman wiped her hands on her apron. "I'm Tessa, by the way."

"Tessa Whitmore." The name clicked it all into place. Jenna remembered her from a reality TV show. "You were on *Order Up: Las Vegas!*"

"Feels like a lifetime ago," Tessa admitted.

"I'm Jenna. I rooted for you from the first episode." Jenna didn't care that she was fangirling. Watching that cooking competition had gotten her through one of her roughest rough patches with Whitney. Binging the reality TV show helped Jenna tune out her sister's negativity long enough to finish an overdue book in her most popular series. One her publishing company threatened *not* to publish if she didn't get it turned in *asap*. "I still think you should've won. Especially after that snake sabotaged you and got you kicked off the show. I was so happy when they brought you back for the finale."

"You know what? I'm going to save you *two* muffins. Stop by the kitchen when you get back, Jenna."

Before she dashed out into the rain, Jenna pulled her hood up and switched her phone to silent mode.

If she didn't need the GPS to navigate to the restaurant, she'd have turned her phone off and left it in the nightstand drawer.

The drive to Moosecakes was surprisingly short. Had it not been for the weather, she might've walked. *Or accepted the ride Cody offered.* But Jenna was nervous enough about spending the day with the man who made her heart flutter in a way it never had. She needed these spare minutes to compose herself before she met up with him again.

Jenna shuffled through the influx of texts, finding the one that wasn't from her sister or part of the group text from earlier.

**Cody:** I'm inside.

The diner-style restaurant, complete with a counter in the middle with bar-style seating, was packed. Checkered black and white flooring traveled throughout the space. A variety of moose-themed decorations from professional photographs to tin-cut designs covered the walls, sprinkles of Alaskan license plates filling in most gaps.

Dozens of curious gazes lifted to the newcomer, making Jenna wish she'd waited to turn down her rain-splattered hood. She scanned the restaurant twice before she caught Cody's wave from a corner booth.

"Is this place always so busy?" she asked, slipping into the booth opposite Cody.

"Pretty much." He slid a steaming cup of coffee toward her as she shrugged out of her jacket. "Wasn't sure if you were a coffee drinker."

"On occasion." Jenna tended to drink the bitter liquid for two reasons. Either she was on a deadline and in desperate need of caffeine or she was chilled to the bone. She dumped a couple of creamer and sugar packets into her cup and stirred.

"You need something besides coffee?" a waitress asked, appearing at the table with a nearly empty coffee pot.

"Apple juice?" Jenna asked.

"You got it. You two ready to order?"

"I haven't seen a menu."

Cody lifted one from behind the condiment holder and set it in front of her. "This place is famous for their moose-shaped pancakes. Kids and adults alike go nuts for them. They're not just fun, they're delicious."

"I don't like pancakes."

Both Cody and the waitress did a double take. "You don't like pancakes?" Cody repeated the words slowly, his eyebrows drawn in confusion. "As in *all* pancakes? Because these are made from scratch. I've been all around the world and never had better."

Jenna scanned the omelet section of the menu, unsurprised by his reaction. She'd never met another person who didn't like pancakes. "Can I have the Denali omelet with wheat toast?" she directed at the waitress.

"Of course, hun." She looked at Cody. "Usual for you?"

Cody nodded.

"Your mom is an amazing cook—especially where breakfast is concerned—yet you have a regular order here?" Jenna shook her head. "If I had your mom, I'd never eat out again."

"Your mom doesn't like to cook?" Cody guessed.

Jenna shrugged, unable to remember who did the cooking when she was growing up. She remembered a lot of meals out of a cereal box or can. Certainly nothing to rave about. "I guess not." After a sip of coffee, she explained, "My mom passed away when I was nine." She hated that the older she got, the less she seemed to remember about the part of her life that included her mom.

"I'm sorry to hear that. I can't imagine."

"It was a long time ago." If Jenna wasn't careful, she'd get herself all choked up with emotions. The last thing she planned to do was turn into a sobbing mess in front of Cody. "After breakfast, what's our next stop?"

"Eager to be rid of me?" The teasing twinkle in his sea-green eyes was dangerous.

"You're the one who has a plane to catch." But yes, Jenna *was* eager. The sooner she got the keys to Grandpa's cabin, the sooner she could send in that two-week notice and decide where home would be. "You never told me what's in Maui."

"A new TV show."

"You're a stuntman, right?"

"Did Haylee or Laurel tell you that?"

Jenna sipped on her coffee, enjoying only the warmth it provided. There wasn't enough creamer in this diner to sweeten it to her impossible standards. "I may have dragged that detail out of a sibling, but I won't tell you which one." Though she guessed all on her own when they first met, yesterday she had asked more than a few questions about the specifics.

"Haylee."

"Don't you ever worry about getting hurt?" Jenna asked, remembering how many stories Grandpa shared about stuntmen—and women—he'd watched botch a stunt and break bones. "One slip and you could end up paralyzed for life. Or dead."

"I've broken a couple bones," Cody admitted. "Cracked three ribs once. That wasn't fun. But it comes with the territory. I know the risks involved."

Jenna kept her expression blank, but she was surprised nonetheless by his nonchalant attitude about a profession that could result in an early death. "She doesn't want you to go, you know. Haylee."

"It's the same every year."

"Except this time, it's *three* years. No time off that isn't for an emergency." Haylee had been more than forthcoming with the details while they scrubbed and hosed off kayaks. She preferred having her family close. She seemed nervous to navigate life without Cody around, but why, Jenna hadn't pinned down. Even without him, the girl still had a ton of family around. "What kind of TV show films that way? I've never heard of such a thing."

"One that's already been signed for five seasons, as long as they're filmed back-to-back. It's all about instant gratification these days." Cody leaned back in his seat as the waitress set plates in front of them. His was stacked with three pancakes shaped to look like a moose's face peering at you. Somehow, the chef had managed to cook a three-piece pancake as one connected work of art. *Fascinating.*

"Can I get you anything else?" the waitress asked. "Besides more coffee?"

Jenna shook her head, eager to cut into her omelet. It was a relief to feel hungry again. All the stress and tension of day-to-day life, coupled with grief over the loss of her grandpa, had robbed her for months of any voracious appetite. Which made Whitney's comment about losing five pounds all the more ridiculous. Jenna had lost eight over the course of the summer. Any more and she'd look unhealthy.

"Wait, we need a picture," Cody said before the waitress hurried away. He handed over his phone, slid their plates close together, and leaned over the table. "Just a quick one, please?"

"I can't get you both in the frame," the waitress apologized after a look behind her. Another couple of inches and she'd back right into a full table.

Cody was up out of his seat and sliding into Jenna's before she had time to register what happened. Her thigh pressed against his as he draped an arm around her. Warmth radiated throughout her as dozens of butterflies fluttered to life in her belly. "Say Moosecakes."

"I'm not saying Moosecakes."

"When in Rome."

"This is definitely not Rome," Jenna answered between clenched teeth for the sake of the picture.

"Hope one of these works for you all." The waitress gave Cody a lingering look as she handed his phone back. One that could mean she was interested in him for herself or applauding him for dining with another woman in public. It'd be easy to mistake them as on a date. Jenna should've realized sooner he had *heartbreaker* written all over him.

Despite that nugget of knowledge, Jenna felt the absence of Cody when he returned to his own side. She blamed the rainy-day chill for enjoying the warmth he so easily provided. "When's the last time you had a serious girlfriend?"

"Jealous?"

Jenna nearly choked on the first bite of her Denali omelet, which would've been a shame considering how delicious it was. "I can point out three women who've been eyeing you like the whipped topping on your pancakes since I walked in the door." Jenna swallowed a bite. "Make that four."

"Thought we'd hit Willamina's Big Dipper for lunch," Cody said, avoiding Jenna's question completely. She let it go temporarily, but she was too curious about this man who'd befriended her grandpa to drop it indefinitely. "We can also get some shopping in since it's raining."

"Shopping?" Saying the word aloud make Jenna shudder.

"Number twelve." He slid his phone across the table, displaying the photo he'd taken of the handwritten list last night. He'd zoomed in to the twelfth item on the list. "Make Jenna buy something frivolous for herself at Forget Me Not."

"No." Another trait about herself that her sister couldn't stand. "I don't do shopping."

Cody smirked, a smudge of whipped cream lifting with one corner of his mouth. Jenna hated to admit how goofily attractive he was in this very moment. "Well, today you do."

"Suppose there's no point in arguing?"

"None whatsoever."

It didn't matter how guarded she wanted to keep her heart, or that the man across the booth would be on an island far away for three whole years. It didn't matter that half a dozen women in the café couldn't keep their eyes off him. Jenna already knew she was in trouble when it came to Cody Evans.

# CHAPTER FIVE

Cody

Cody parked in front of the local gift shop that sat separate from most of the downtown shops. The Forget Me Not was perched on top of a hill, offering its customers a spectacular view of the bay, except when it was foggy and rainy like today.

He unclipped his seat belt but left the engine running. "I have to make a quick call. Go ahead. I'll meet you inside." They'd carpooled from the restaurant, agreeing to knock one more item off the list together before they went back for Graham.

"Is this really necessary?" Jenna looked as though she'd swallowed a lemon.

As antsy as Cody was to call his booking agent before Holden heard about his change in travel plans on Instagram or whatever social media platform

Haylee was favoring today, his obligation to Eddie took priority. "If your grandpa put this on the list, it means something."

"Like what?"

Cody reread the numbered item, contemplating it for several seconds. "Like you don't ever do anything for yourself."

"I do plenty for myself."

"Oh, really?"

"Yes, *really*."

"Name the last thing you did for yourself, with absolutely no one else in mind." He watched her lips part and close multiple times as her vacant stare at the dashboard seemed to search for an out-of-reach answer.

"I moved out of my sister's basement."

Cody let his gaze linger, flirting with the thought of getting lost in those dark, milk-chocolatey eyes. "That was *your* choice? You moved out one hundred percent because *you* wanted to?"

"Well, not exactly," Jenna admitted, avoiding eye contact. "But it was *very* satisfying to pack up that trailer and sneak it to Alaska."

Because Cody was afraid she'd realize she over-shared and clam back up, he didn't pick apart her comment with his many questions. It shouldn't matter that Jenna might move to Sunset Ridge permanently when Cody wasn't going to be around anyway. "But the reason you packed the trailer was because your sister wanted you out?"

"Okay, fine. You caught me. I don't do things for myself all that often. Used to be painting and creating stories, but now that I'm constantly on one deadline or another, that too is to please someone else." She zipped up her jacket and set her hand on the door handle. "Don't be long. I'm not one of those slow-browser shoppers."

Cody nodded, unable to tear his gaze away from Jenna until she disappeared through the gift shop entrance. He didn't dare dissect what he was feeling for a woman he hardly knew. That would only lead to complications he didn't have room for in his life. He'd designed things that way on purpose.

He scrolled through his phone until he landed on Holden's number. His booking agent was going to have a hay day with the news, but Cody had already switched his flight. He wasn't switching it back.

"Cody. Did you get into Maui early? How's the view from your back porch? I bet the sunset is just breathtaking."

"Still in Alaska."

"But your bags are packed, right? Saw one of your sisters tag you in that family photo on Instagram. Looks like your shop's all tucked in for the winter." Cody rarely called Holden unless he was looking for a new gig or needed to clarify contract terms. "Weather forecast looks great. No storms along the West Coast." Holden was Cody's first and only agent since he got into stunts. He knew when Holden sensed something was wrong but was avoiding the elephant in the room as long as he could.

"I'm going to be a few days late," Cody said, ripping off the proverbial Band-Aid. "Had something personal come up."

"Define a few days."

"New flight gets to Maui Sunday morning."

"One day before filming starts?" Holden sounded less than impressed. "You do know how many other stuntmen wanted this job, right? There's still three guys with bags packed just waiting for a call to take your spot."

The show, based on a bestselling romantic suspense series of books, was guaranteed to be a massive hit before the cast was even selected. The response in picking up the series for TV was unlike anything the industry had ever seen. Multiple networks entered a bidding war, and the winner promised five full seasons in three years. That contract length for film work was hard to come by, and Cody had been lucky to be selected as the male lead's stunt double.

"I'll be there Sunday," Cody said, his gazing flickering to the gift shop window as Jenna walked by it. "I've already read over the script for the pilot. I know what's expected of me. It's nothing I can't handle." Before Holden could get too upset, Cody added, "The contract requires me to be on the set next Monday at six a.m. and that's exactly where I'll be.

Can you let them know I'll miss the dinner the night before?"

"Sure. Don't be a minute late. I can't help you if you are."

Holden ended the call before Cody could reassure him he had nothing to worry about. He'd made other last-minute deadlines, but never for a commitment this big. One that promised to open doors for him in the future. At the end of this series, he could practically hand select any stunt project he wanted, on *his* terms. Which meant he could spend more time in Alaska—at *home*.

Cody scrolled through his contacts until he found Sadie's number, his finger hovering over the call button. But before he could tap it with his finger, he spotted movement beside the log-cabin shop. Ed emerged through the trees at the back of the building, sauntering toward the parking lot. The moose stopped shy of the gift shop window and stared at Cody. Another foot and Jenna would have a clear view of their most famous local celebrity.

"That's some luck," he said, unable to hide his smile as he cautiously pushed open his door. "Number five, here we come."

Ed tilted his head, massive antlers going lopsided.

"Don't move, Ed." He kept his steps toward the gift shop entrance slow and calm as to not aggravate the beast. Getting a selfie *with* Ed would be tricky. But maybe in this one instance, having an additional witness would be proof enough. He'd spotted the owner Ava Young working. She'd vouch for them for sure. "Seriously Ed, do me a solid and stay right there."

He quickly slipped inside, calling for Jenna. "Come quick. Ed's outside."

She stared back with drawn eyebrows. "What?"

"The moose." When she still didn't seem to register what he was saying, he added, "Number five on the list."

"Oh!" She set whatever gadget she'd been eyeing on the counter and hurried to the door. Ava followed her. Even the locals got excited to see Ed when he came around.

At the door, he held out his arm. "Go slow. He's right around the corner. You don't want to startle him. Hard to finish a bucket list after you've been trampled by a moose."

Cody's lame joke won him a crooked smile and an amused headshake. He went last, closing the door gently behind him. Ed was the tamest moose he'd ever encountered, except for the few they kept at the Anchorage Zoo. But he was still a wild creature easily rattled by loud noises.

"I'm going to try to take a selfie—"

"Cody."

"Don't know if it'll turn out. Ed's not one for pictures—"

"Cody!" Jenna's stern tone snapped him to attention. "I don't see a moose."

Cody's excitement plummeted in a single heartbeat. He peered around the corner, finding hoof prints in the dirt—but no Ed. Cody circled the building, certain the beast couldn't have gone far. Much of the fog had cleared and the trees in nearby residential yards were thin in most places. But Cody couldn't even make out the crunch of leaves to give him a clue where the moose wandered off to in so short a time. "You've got to be kidding me," he muttered when he made it back to the front.

"Are you sure it was a moose?" Jenna asked.

"It wasn't an alley cat." He scrubbed a hand over his face, releasing any tension he felt over the near-miss before his hand dropped. They still had five days to see Ed. Considering Cody had spotted him twice in two days, the odds were in their favor.

"Ed's a finicky creature, capable of running up to thirty-five miles per hour when he chooses," Ava said, holding the door open for Jenna and Cody. "If he wants you to see him, believe me, you'll see him."

"Ava's one of the many in Sunset Ridge who believes Ed is a matchmaker," Cody explained to Jenna, hoping she'd find the story amusing. But if she read into it, he didn't seem to mind that thought either. Even if he didn't believe in wild matchmaking mammals.

Jenna laughed instantly at his comment, but her expression dropped when she noticed Ava wasn't joining in. She looked back and forth between the store owner and Cody. "Wait. You're serious?"

"I'm pretty sure Ed had a hand in me ending up

with my husband," Ava said sincerely. "Two of my best friends have found their way to their soulmates too, all thanks to Ed's inconvenient appearances. He may be a moose, but I tell you, he knows when someone needs to slow down so love can catch up." Ava looked at Cody. "Tell me Ed's not the reason your sister Laurel gave Chase a second chance?"

"That's up for debate." Cody caught Jenna eyeing a rotating rack beside the front counter. "Find something you like?"

"Yep." Jenna held out a brass keychain in the shape of Alaska. "Get over here so we can take the photo."

"No."

"What do you mean *no?*"

Ava watched with amusement from behind the checkout counter, so Cody enlisted her help. "Ava, if you had to pick out something from your charming gift shop for yourself just because, would you pick out a simple keychain?"

"I prefer the clothing section myself. Lots of beautiful scarves perfect for fall."

"Hey, no fair ganging up on me," Jenna interjected, holding her prize up so it dangled from her finger. "I happen to like this keychain."

Cody wondered if money was the issue but was not about to ask such an invasive question. "I'm going to bet when your grandpa made this list, *he* planned to buy you whatever you picked out." He hooked his finger through the loop of the keychain, grazing Jenna's soft palm in the process. He pretended it didn't affect him, but the zing of electricity traveled quickly up his arm and warmed his chest to life. "Your grandpa would never have agreed to buy you a keychain." He turned his attention to the owner and said, "Ava, put whatever Jenna wants on my tab. But only if she picks out something splurge-worthy."

When Jenna hadn't moved from the keychain display, Cody dropped both hands onto her shoulders and steered her to the women's boutique clothing section.

"Every piece of clothing in the store is made in Alaska," Ava explained. "Many of the pieces are one of a kind."

Cautiously, Jenna thumbed through a rack of silk shirts, some solid, some with gentle floral patterns. Cody could imagine her in any one of them, but Jenna wore a hesitant expression. "Ava, do you have a dressing room?"

"I do."

"Great. Jenna would like to try on some shirts."

"Hey—"

"If you want me to take that picture, you'll have to put some actual effort into this." He lifted three different choices off the rack and held them out to Jenna. "If you don't like any of them, you don't have to get one. You *are* supposed to buy something you want, after all."

"I want the keychain."

"No, you don't."

"Did anyone ever tell you that you're frustrating?" Jenna asked with narrowed eyes.

Cody pretended to think about it for a minute, then shook his head. "Nope. You'd be the first."

With an *ugh*, Jenna shut the dressing room door behind her.

"Cody Evans, do you have an actual *girlfriend?*" Ava asked, her tone barely above an excited whisper. He could understand her curiosity, considering the last serious girlfriend he'd had—yes, he'd given Jenna's question serious thought, not that he'd let her know that—was when he was seventeen and still in high school. Ten years ago. He was careful to avoid dates when he was home unless he could take a woman out in a neighboring town, for *this* exact reason. The small-town folks loved to speculate, especially on love lives.

"No, she's just a friend."

A mischievous twinkle in Ava's eyes revealed she didn't believe him. Before he could set the record straight, though, the dressing room door opened.

"I don't *hate* this one," Jenna admitted, her lips contorting as if she were fighting a grin she didn't want him to see. She looked radiant even without the full smile. The burnt-orange long-sleeved top with smocked cuffs seemed to be made for Jenna's slim figure. It wasn't just flattering on her, it was stunning.

"You look amazing," Ava said sincerely, moving from behind the counter. Making a brief stop at a rotating tower of necklaces, she selected one and approached Jenna. "Here, let me put this on. I think it'll pair nicely with that top."

The sparkle in Jenna's eyes when she looked at herself in the mirror was unmistakable. "I actually like this."

"Like it?" Ava teased. "That look says you're madly in love."

Cody didn't remember moving his feet, but suddenly, he was standing beside Jenna in the mirror. He draped an arm over her shoulder, softly squeezing her against him. He wished he could read her better, because then he might understand why the sight she saw in the mirror now was so surprising to her. "You look ravishing."

Jenna raised an eyebrow at him. "Nobody says *ravishing* anymore."

"I just did." Because the physical contact was having unexpected effects on his pulse, he dropped his arm. "What do you think? Have you found your special thing?"

"Do I have to pick *one*?" Jenna asked, twisting the heart-shaped pendant with her fingers.

"Of course not."

"But the list said—"

"The point of the list is to push you outside your comfort zone. Haven't you figured that out already?" Cody looked to Ava. "Ring them both up. You should have my credit card on file. Oh, and toss a couple of your homemade dog treats in there, too." The Forget Me Not was the store he frequented online when he was in other parts of the world and wanted to give Alaskan-made gifts to new friends. If his mom ever knew how much business he gave Ava, she might have a heart attack.

"You don't have to pay for this," Jenna said from the dressing room door. "I have money."

"I really enjoyed your grandpa's company, but I don't need his ghost haunting me." Cody made a shooing motion. "Get changed. We'll grab Graham, then head to lunch at Willamina's Big Dipper."

"Oh, The Dipper's closed on Mondays during the off season," Ava said after the dressing room door closed. "Willamina just posted her new hours last week."

"Good to know." Cody pulled his phone out again while he waited for Jenna to change, but before he could pull up the list, Sadie's name appeared on the screen.

**Sadie:** Dinner at Bear Tooth?
**Sadie:** What time does your flight leave tomorrow?
**Sadie:** I have to work, but I'll take off early.

Cody might be the only Evans sibling who truly understood Sadie, which was why he knew a call was necessary if he didn't want his phone to explode with dozens of frantic texts. But she sent him to voicemail on the second ring.

He let out a groan before the beep. "Sadie, this is your favorite brother. Call me back."

**Sadie:** In a meeting.
**Sadie:** I'll see you tomorrow.
**Sadie:** Just tell me what time???

"Something the matter?" Jenna asked as she carried the folded blouse and pendant to the checkout counter. He didn't hear her approach, but now that she stood beside him, her cinnamon-vanilla scent swarmed around him.

"Sadie," he said, scrubbing a hand once over his face. "The sister you didn't get to meet."

"Everything okay?"

"Yeah. Just . . . typical Sadie." Though Haylee was the sibling who was the most vocal about wanting Cody to give up his three-year-long gig and stay in Sunset Ridge, Sadie was struggling the most *internally* with his departure. Without him around, she felt she didn't have an ally in the family. A point she'd emphasized on dozens of occasions since he told his family about his longest gig. "Change of plans."

"You could grab a pizza at Warren's Sea Shack," Ava suggested, wrapping the pendant in tissue paper and sealing it with a store sticker.

"Seafood on pizza?" Jenna asked, her nose wrinkled.

"Yeah, it's not really my thing either. But lots of people love it." Ava slid a handled paper bag across the counter. "Or you could check out Whitmore Patio. I think Tessa adjusted the hours for the off season. She might be open since The Dipper isn't."

"Great idea," Cody said, thanking Ava and handing her his phone to snap a picture to satisfy the photographic evidence requirement for item number twelve. "If Sophie's working, we can knock at least one more thing off the list today. Her husband's the author we need to track down."

# CHAPTER SIX

Jenna

For the first time in three long months, Jenna felt the feather's nudge of inspiration tickling her senses. A fresh idea for a story was forming in wisps. She didn't know much beyond that the main character starring in her new children's book series would be a moose, but it felt like a promising start.

"Is that a smile?" Cody teased from across the round table. Whitmore Patio had moved indoors now that the peak tourist season was finished and the weather favored cold, rainy days like today rather than sunny patio-friendly ones. They chose a table by a window covered in streaks of rain.

"What? I smile."

"Not all that often."

Jenna reached for her goblet of ice water. "I

haven't had a lot to smile about since I lost Grandpa." To her surprise, the admission didn't make tears instantly prick the corners of her eyes. It *did* unsurprisingly cause her chest to tighten and her pulse to double in an irrational panic. She couldn't imagine a day she wouldn't feel *some* pinch of loss.

"Eddie was such an incredible guy," Cody said, awe in his tone. "He was a talented screenwriter, which you no doubt know. But he was such a kind, interesting, spectacular human being." The warm way he spoke of her grandpa brought her unexpected comfort. "I met him for the first time in Barbados, four years ago. But I had the pleasure of working on three different movie sets with him. He's the only screenwriter I've ever actually met. They don't hang around the set much. Eddie told me he got inspired to write something new by watching the stunts."

"He told me that, too." Jenna remembered the conversation fondly. She'd been eleven, drawing a magical forest at the kitchen table. Grandpa was cooking because Whitney was working a double shift. "I asked him how he came up with his ideas one night while he was making dinner."

"Did you ever get to go with him on set?" Cody asked, those dangerously tempting sea-green eyes sparkling with excitement.

"Yeah, a few times." Jenna smiled fondly at the memories from her childhood. "The older I got, though, the less I went. Never seemed to be any time. Between my full-time desk job and constant deadlines with my editor, I had a lot of reasons to stay home. Not a lot of movies filmed in Indiana, you know." It'd also been easier to say no so that Whitney wouldn't get bent out of shape about Jenna being gone. Though underneath her sister's snide comments was a jealous girl who messed up her opportunity to be on a movie set ever again.

"What's that look about?" Cody's tone was gentle enough, but she felt the press for information that always made her slam her walls into place.

"What look?"

"You two ready to order?" Sophie Grant asked sweetly as she approached their table. "Tessa made an amazing halibut corn chowder, but it's going fast."

"That sounds really good," Jenna said, relief at the interruption. "Sign me up for that."

"I'll take the same," Cody said. "And some of that cornbread if that's on the menu today." He looked at Jenna, his crooked smile returning the normalcy to their conversation. "She makes it from scratch. Don't tell my mom, but it's better than hers."

"Cornbread for you, too?" Sophie asked Jenna.

"Yes, please."

"Say, Sophie, is your husband on a deadline right now?"

She rolled her eyes playfully. "He's *always* on a deadline."

"Do you think he'd be upset if we popped by after lunch? I'd like to get Jenna an autographed copy of one of his books."

"I think he'd be fine with that."

"Thank you." Jenna spotted the curiosity dancing in Sophie's eyes. She suspected they were on a date. The best thing to do would be to clear that misconception up right now before Sophie hurried back to the kitchen. Cody knew it as well as she did. Instead, he stayed silent. And Jenna wasn't about to delay their halibut corn chowder in case they were nearly out.

"I'll call the house after I get your soup. Caroline's off from school today—parent-teacher conferences. I'll have her set one out for him to sign." She looked at Jenna. "Any particular book you'd like?"

"Surprise us," Cody said before Jenna could give some generic answer. She couldn't even recall *who* this author was from the list, much less if she'd heard of him. Might be that Grandpa got a kick out of meeting another author and thought she'd find that neat as well. Or it was a hint she should consider moving to Alaska—*see, another author writes up here!*

"How do you know I don't *have* all of his books?" Jenna asked.

Cody lifted his glass as he met her gaze, and her heart fluttered. She understood why half the women in this town were practically falling over themselves to get Cody to turn his head their way. One look in those eyes was all it took to be lost to his effortless charm. She'd witnessed the phenomenon a few times, even if he seemed oblivious. Which she didn't believe was anything more than an act to spare their feelings. "What's his name?" Cody asked.

"Who?" *Oh, he means the author. Might've helped if I'd read the list closer.* She reached for the folded paper in her jacket pocket. "It's—"

"No cheating," he said, grabbing the list from her before she could unfold it. His fingertips grazed the side of her hand, causing those pesky butterflies in her stomach to get a little wild. Not that she'd ever let him know that.

Instead, Jenna narrowed her eyes at him. But the severity from earlier glares didn't find this one. She was warming up to him. A problem for both of them if it kept on this way. And yet, she couldn't find the good sense to be bothered by that. "Hardly seems fair."

"Denver's expecting you after lunch," Sophie said, returning with chowder and cornbread. "If he's still in sweatpants, just ignore that. He's on this whole roll-out-of-bed-and write-first-thing kick. He's been getting his words twice as fast, so I don't pester him about it."

"Thanks, Sophie," Cody said before she whisked away to help another table, leaving him to turn a curious gaze to Jenna. "Do you write in your pajamas, too?"

"Used to." She tore off a corner of her cornbread, silently mourning the glory days when she'd draft an entire story in a day wearing her favorite pajama pants. Those were the days her excitement was too high to let even Whitney kill her good mood. "Wow, this is *really* good. The food alone might make me stay in Sunset Ridge. My sister'd be horrified if I told her how much I've been eating since I got here." Jenna couldn't help the malicious smile that crept across her lips as she imagined Whitney's appalled expression. Maybe then she'd accept that Jenna wasn't going to the wedding. "Did you know Tessa— the same one from *Order Up: Las Vegas* by the way— makes amazing white chocolate raspberry muffins?"

"Your sister sounds . . . interesting."

Jenna sputtered a laugh that lifted her shoulders with it. "Let's just say my family is *nothing* like yours."

"Why don't you write in your pajamas anymore?"

*Because I'd have to actually write to do that.* "Writing's been hard since Grandpa died," she said, staring into her chowder bowl, feeling her spirits drain. One inspired idea about a moose didn't automatically mean she was cured of her grief-induced writer's block. "I write upbeat children's books full of magic and adventure. I guess lately I've stopped believing in magic. And the only adventure I was up for before the very long road trip to Alaska was a Netflix binge day under the covers. Graham was quite the fan of ordering in and snuggling in bed all day."

"Can't imagine your grandpa would want you to stop believing in magic."

"I know he wouldn't." She parted her lips to say more, but instead helped herself to a spoonful of chowder. She was having an easier time talking about her grandpa without breaking down into a sobbing mess, but she was nearing her limit. "We have time for anything else on the list after we get an autograph?"

Cody opened the list he'd confiscated from her, browsing it as he finished his lunch. "We'll have to wait for tomorrow to grab halibut tacos at Warren's. He only makes them on Tuesdays during the off season."

"What about that Bear Glacier kayaking?"

"Waiting for a call back from a buddy." Cody emptied his soup bowl and followed the last spoonful with a healthy gulp of water. "That one's a little more involved."

"Because you packed all your kayaks away for the winter?" she guessed.

"I *always* have a couple kayaks handy at my parents' place. They bought me my own shed for my birthday one year."

"Wow, that was generous."

Cody slipped his card out of his wallet and set it on the edge of the table. "I was taking up an entire garage stall, which considering I'm gone most of the winter, was getting on their nerves." He pulled out a vibrating phone, glanced at the screen, and dropped it back in his pocket. "We need more than a couple of kayaks to complete number nine. Weather's looking good for Wednesday if Liam's available to fly out there."

"Fly?" Jenna felt the bottom of her stomach drop out.

"It's a two-day hike otherwise."

*Jenna, you can fly on a plane this one time.*

Cody collected his returned card. Jenna tried to pay for breakfast earlier, but he'd made it very clear he didn't want her grandpa to haunt him. It was a hard habit to break, allowing someone else to pay for things and not tense up at what might be expected in return. She'd spent a lifetime feeling she *owed* Whitney for all the sacrifices she'd made for Jenna. She didn't want to feel that way ever again—for anyone.

When she said as much to Cody, he shook his head. "Are you sure this is your *sister* you're talking about?"

"Only one I've got," Jenna muttered. "Let me grab Graham. I want to take him out before the rain picks back up."

In the room, Jenna closed the door and sank against it. "Hey there, Graham Cracker." As she slid to the floor, she gathered him in a hug on her lap. He was the world's best snuggler. "You been napping, buddy?"

He answered with a cute half yawn, half moan noise, followed by an eager butt wiggle.

Because she needed a few minutes before she returned to Cody, Jenna decided to check her phone —a decision she instantly regretted. If she thought Whitney's texts were out of control this morning, it was nothing compared to the influx she'd gotten since she left the lodge. "Thirty-two texts, Whitney?" she groaned. Apparently, giving her sister a heads-up about her lack of cell signal today was code for *bombard me with texts*.

The last text was the one that made guilt twist in her stomach.

**Whitney:** Remember who took you in rent-free while you went to that fancy illustration school. For TWO years. You owe me.

It would be so much easier to cut ties with her overbearing sister if Whitney simply forgot Jenna existed. But no. Her poison of choice was the constant reminder that Jenna wouldn't have the publishing success she did today without her sister allowing her to move into her basement while she immersed herself in learning from illustrating masters and creating entire worlds in books.

Reluctantly, Jenna scrolled through the texts. Ninety percent of them were about the wedding and all the tasks that Whitney had put on her plate without asking. It was bad enough that her sister was marrying a real jerk and couldn't see past his good looks and fat bank account to realize it. Quite another to be strong-armed into planning so much of it.

"Graham, you like Alaska, right?" she asked the dog, rubbing both his ears the way he liked. "I like

Alaska. We should just stay here." He tilted his head at her, making her feel that if he could raise an eyebrow, he'd be doing it right now. "No, it has nothing to do with that handsome—"

A rap at her door made her eyes double in size. How loud had she been talking out loud to her dog? "Jenna, you in there?" The sound of Cody's voice made her heart race in ways it never had on any date. *Especially the ones Whitney set up.*

"Coming." She hopped to her feet, clipped Graham's leash to his collar, and opened the door.

Instantly, her traitorous dog leaned against both of Cody's legs, demanding pets as he melted into his new bestie. "Guess your family and your adoring fan club of single women aren't the only ones who are going to miss you while you're hanging out on the beach." Jenna locked the door behind her and led them to the back door.

"I don't have a fan club," Cody said nonchalantly. "I'm just a stunt double."

"Oh, please." Jenna rolled her eyes with exaggeration to get her point across. "If I had a dollar for every woman who practically swooned in your presence, I'd be staying here for free." She let Graham sniff and explore to his heart's content until he ran in a bunch of circles and picked *the* spot.

"Tell me more about this sister of yours," Cody asked innocently.

Jenna shook her head, despite the burning urge to vent to someone. "That's not on the list." She didn't have any close friends back in Indiana. The girls at work were also friends with Whitney, considering her sister had helped Jenna get that job, too. *Just one more thing to hold over me. How did I not see that coming?* "Think it's done raining?"

"Definitely not."

"Sorry, Graham. Looks like we'll have to save that W-A-L-K for tomorrow."

Jenna, following Cody's instructions, drove them the few blocks to a two-story house on a corner lot. They caught a glimpse of a man seated at a desk in a corner window. Jenna envied the way he looked lost in what she could only assume was his story.

She'd never be a novelist. That much was certain. But she loved getting lost in the magic of creating just the same.

A young girl, maybe seven or eight, answered the door. She was the spitting image of Sophie. "Denver, they're here!" she announced eagerly, holding the door open and stepping back to let them inside.

A few moments later, a man dressed in sweatpants and a three-day-old beard stepped into the hall to greet them. "Hey, Cody," the man greeted. "And you must be Jenna." Denver extended his hand. "It's nice to meet you. Are you a . . . friend of Cody's?" he guessed.

"Denver, this is Jenna Kingsley."

Denver studied Jenna an uncomfortable amount of time. "Eddie Kingsley's granddaughter. How did I not see it right away?" With each person she met,

Jenna was more and more surprised by how many people in this small town remembered her grandpa. It made her question just how many trips he made. Surely it was more than the three he claimed. "Please, come into my office."

"Can I get you something to drink?" the little girl asked, sounding much too mature for her tiny frame. "We have water, milk, and apple juice."

"Apple juice?" Jenna repeated, unable to hide her excitement.

"It's my favorite."

"Mine, too."

"Caroline, why don't you grab two waters and an apple juice." Denver looked to Cody. "Unless you want coffee? I've been trying to cut back on caffeine. It was murder for a few weeks, but now that I've broken the habit, I have a lot more energy for writing."

"Water's good."

Slipping into a chair off to the side of a massive L-shaped desk, Jenna noticed a stack of books. She glimpsed the spines pointed in her direction, shock hitting her. "Wait, you're Denver *Grant*. As in the insanely popular mystery writer, Denver Grant." Jenna wasn't sure why the name on the list hadn't jumped out at her before, but now that the dots were connected, her pulse was going crazy. "I've read every one of your books." By read, she meant she'd binged his entire series last Christmas. And when his latest came out over the summer, she called in sick to work and devoured it in one day. Whitney had been livid when she caught Jenna wrapped up in a book, but even her wrath had been worth it.

"Probably not the newest one," Denver said, holding up a paperback copy of a book she'd been anticipating for weeks. A banner across the cover marked it as a *proof copy not for sale*.

"Jenna writes and illustrates children's books." Jenna vaguely heard Cody speaking as Denver handed over the proof copy of his newest book. One that wasn't due to release for two more weeks. Her fingers trembled with excitement. Though the previous book included a satisfyingly solved mystery, there'd been one doozey of a cliffhanger. The temptation to start reading right now tugged at her.

"You write *and* illustrate?" Denver asked. "That's impressive."

"She's J.A. Kingsley," Caroline announced as she carried bottled beverages into the office. The sweet girl offered the most adorable beaming smile. "I have all your books, too."

"Caroline." She vaguely remembered signing a set of books last summer at her grandpa's request. "*You're* Caroline."

The girl nodded eagerly.

"It's a pleasure to meet you."

"Are you writing any new books yet?"

From the intelligent way this little girl carried herself, Jenna wondered if Caroline might've outgrown picture books. "Soon, I hope."

Jenna felt Cody's gaze flicker to her more than once as Caroline rambled a mile a minute with adoration for every book she'd read, and each time she felt him looking, it made her nerves tingle. She blamed it on the excitement of meeting not only her favorite author, but one of her biggest fans.

"We better let you get back to writing," Jenna said when the conversation lulled. She was eager to find a notepad and scribble down her newest ideas. Maybe what she'd needed—more than meeting her favorite author—was to talk to an insightful young girl who renewed Jenna's spirits and reminded her why she started crafting stories to begin with. "I don't want to be a target if your fans found out I delayed the next release."

"Aren't you forgetting something?" Cody asked, holding up the folded list for her to see.

"Oh, a signed copy. Right." Her entire collection of Denver Grant's books was packed in a box, buried in the back of her trailer. "I have them all, but none of them are *signed*. Do you have a copy of the first in series?"

"Or I could sign this proof copy," Denver offered.

"Of the book that's not even out yet?" Excitement bubbled in her chest, and her fingers tingled with anticipation of owning that special copy. "If you're expecting me to say no, I won't."

Denver grabbed a pen from a *Yoda Best Writer* coffee mug next to his double monitors and flipped open the cover. He scribbled an inscription and handed it over to Jenna. "Just do me a favor. Don't post any spoilers."

"I know better than that. Not trying to become the next murder victim if your fans got a hold of me." She hugged the book to her chest, savoring the good feelings today graced on her. It felt like an eternity since she experienced such happiness. She hoped Cody wouldn't mind setting aside the list for the rest of the day. Right now, all she craved was getting back to her hotel room and writing down all her new ideas. She even had an image in mind for her main moose character. With any luck, she'd have *something* to send her agent soon. As long as she could keep herself from binge-reading Denver's latest book before she did.

Sunset Ridge was quickly making itself the home she never knew she craved. The only problem was the blond-haired guy with the crooked smile and sea-green eyes who was set to leave on a plane in a few days. Would she feel the same about this place without him?

# CHAPTER SEVEN

Cody

"You like her," Haylee declared as Cody bounced his niece in his arms.

He could ignore her for a minute, maybe two. But his youngest sister was the most persistent of the Evans siblings. She wouldn't let up until he gave an answer. He wasn't about to tell her the truth about the way Jenna's dazzling smile made him feel unexplainably complete or how attractive he found the way she wasn't afraid to speak boldly about topics others might tiptoe around.

Instead, he made goofy sounds until Melly giggled in delight.

Man, he'd miss those big blue adoring eyes. This baby girl would be walking soon, and he wouldn't be here to witness those first steps. Sure, his contract would allow him to come home if there was an emergency. But due to the nature of the show, they weren't given enough time off around the holidays to travel anywhere. Maybe he could send his family plane tickets instead.

"Jenna, I mean. You like Jenna."

"She's nice," admitted Cody, relieved it was only the three of them in the house. And one of them couldn't talk yet. "Everyone who meets her likes her. Look at our entire family. They practically adopted her."

"No. You like-like her."

Cody carried Melly to her highchair as Haylee twisted the lid off a small jar of homemade sweet potato puree. Melly went nuts for Nana Beth's recipes. "Do you have a point?" he asked, careful to keep his tone nonchalant. Lately, he was finding it harder to stay calm and collected. It required effort where before it came naturally. Never before had that been a problem. *Until Jenna Kingsley showed up with that letter*. "And before you say stay, I can't."

"It's just a stupid contract," Haylee groaned.

"For the most anticipated TV series possibly ever," Cody pointed out, though the argument didn't even hold as much weight with him as it did a week ago. He loved traveling the world. Exploring between shoots and meeting interesting people. It fed a part of his soul that nothing else could. He got antsy sitting still in one place too long. Yet now he was yearning to put down roots for the first time . . .ever.

Despite that unfamiliar urge, this gig would set him up financially if he did decide to bow out of stunt work.

"If you leave, she'll just end up married to someone else before you come back to visit."

An irrational pang of jealousy took hold of Cody at the thought. He didn't do jealous. He didn't do strong feelings or relationships or anything of the like that required commitment. He preferred living on his own terms, coming and going as he pleased. Never having to worry about a broken heart crushing him. Or him hurting another soul when he broke things off.

Yet the idea of coming back to Sunset Ridge three years later and seeing Jenna with a baby of her own in her lap and wearing a ring he hadn't given her twisted his stomach in knots.

"I can't stay, Haylee. That's career suicide, and you know it."

"Do you hear me complaining? It'd be nice if you actually stayed all winter instead of dropping in for the occasional Christmas Day and leaving two days later. Your worldly gifts are cool and all, but ask anyone in the family. We'd all rather have you *around* than stuff to remember you by."

Haylee handed him the jar and spoon. Melly banged on the highchair tray, her excitement contagious and her appetite ravenous. It reminded him of a comment Jenna made about her sister and eating. He tried to give everyone the benefit of the doubt. Many were misunderstood or acting out because they were hurting. But he wasn't certain he'd like Jenna's sister should he ever meet her.

"What would I do if I stayed here anyway?" Cody played off the question as a joke, but deep down, he hoped his insightful sister, wise beyond her nineteen years, would have an answer.

"You could help Dad out at the store, for one." Their dad promised any of the Evans' siblings a job at the family outdoor outfitters store if ever they needed one, as long as they were willing to work. Sadie had already been fired once and quit before she could be fired the second time. Which reminded him, she hadn't called him back about rescheduling the dinner she was expecting to have with him in Anchorage tonight.

"Any other ideas?"

"You're this extreme adventure person. Be a ski instructor or something."

"We don't have any slopes within fifty miles of Sunset Ridge," he pointed out. "Next idea?"

Haylee stopped in the middle of a spin in the kitchen and stared at him. *Uh-oh.* "You really *are* thinking about staying."

"Thinking about it and actually doing it are two completely different things. Maybe in three years, when this gig is up, I might stick around more." He'd been careful not to confess as much to his family because he didn't want to disappoint them if he changed his mind. He might decide Maui was home and never come back for more than a visit. He and Dad had already had that conversation about the kayak shop, just in case. "Besides, Jenna hasn't decided if she's moving here or not."

"You *do* like-like her." Haylee's eyes sparkled with matchmaking mischief. What had he done?

"Haylee, stay out of it."

"I'm pretty good at these things," she pressed on. "Look at Laurel and Chase. They got back together, didn't they?"

"Your *one* dinner invitation wasn't the reason that happened," he countered. "If you remember, Sadie nearly sabotaged that." He rarely spoke ill of the sibling only he truly understood. But he was grasping at straws.

"You said *secrets* almost kept them apart."

Ah, so he had. "Speaking of secrets, we're overdue to pick up our last conversation." Melly giggled, almost on cue. She was the topic, after all. "You don't have to tell me who the father is if you don't want to, but I think you should tell Melly's dad about the daughter he doesn't know he has."

"It's complicated," Haylee said, instantly losing that sparkle, as she did every time they discussed it. She'd promised him it wasn't someone who was married or anything that disastrous. But she refused to tell him *why* she wanted to keep Melly's father's identity a secret. "I have my reason, Cody. You know I wouldn't do it otherwise."

"Is that what you're going to tell Melly when she's old enough to ask questions about her dad?"

Haylee busied herself in the kitchen, banging cupboard doors, running water, and clanging dirty dishes. Their parents had taken her in with open arms when she came home from college pregnant, and allowed her to live with them in exchange for chores and occasional hours at the store. Including washing dishes, which she hated the most of all.

"Haylee—"

Cody's phone vibrated against the table, causing Melly's eyes to widen with curiosity. Sadie's name flashed across his screen. He could do this—juggle two sisters and a hungry baby at the same time. "Sadie, hey."

"What time are you meeting me tonight?" The indistinguishable chatter of noise in the background made it hard to hear. But he'd bet she wasn't at work. He hoped she hadn't gotten fired again because of the on-again-off-again boyfriend messing with her emotions. One her family thought was long gone.

"I had to change my flight."

"You better not be in Maui right now!" The snappiness in her tone spoke more to desperation than anger. *Ah, so they're off again.*

"I'm at home for a few more days," he said, letting those words sink in before he continued. He waved the sweet potato puree filled spoon around like an airplane, making Melly flash him that heart-melting smile. "Flying out on Saturday now."

"Can I come with you?" she asked with a pitiful laugh that confirmed his suspicions. "I'll do all the cooking and cleaning. I won't be loud or embarrass you in front of your friends. Please, Cody?"

"You know I can't take you with me." This wasn't the first time they'd had a similar conversation. He loved Sadie dearly, but she had a lot of growing up to do. The best he could hope was that the *off again* stuck for good. "But you can come visit in a couple months once I'm settled."

"It'll be a lot harder to hide in your suitcase that way."

"Is that Sadie?" Haylee hollered from the kitchen. "You know, the sister who won't answer the phone when I call?"

"Did Haylee try to call you?" he asked, all too familiar with the referee role. He'd played it most of their lives.

"Maybe."

"Can you call her back?"

"Tomorrow."

"Tell Sadie she needs to be home on Friday afternoon," Haylee added between cupboard bangs. He felt a sliver of guilt for bringing up Melly's father. The topic always put her in a bad mood. Maybe he could make up for it by inviting her to Warren's Sea Shack when he met Jenna for dinner. "If she wants to know why, she can *call* me."

"Text me the time you want to meet Saturday," Sadie said.

"Are you going to call Haylee?"

"Tomorrow."

"Call her tomorrow or you're not visiting Maui." It was an empty threat and they both knew it. Cody wasn't convinced his sister wouldn't just show up in a couple of weeks with packed bags and announce she spent her last dollar on the flight to Hawaii.

"Sure, okay. Let me know about Saturday." Sadie ended the call before he could say more. He might be the only one who understood their directionless sister, but that didn't mean he was all that great at getting through to her.

"She's not going to call me," Haylee muttered. "You know it as well as I do."

"Want to go to Warren's with me for halibut tacos?"

"Is that a list item?" Haylee asked, instantly perking.

"Does that matter?"

She rolled her eyes. "I should've just asked if Jenna was going to be there."

Cody realized his mistake too late. His act of kindness would offer his incredibly insightful little sister time to observe things he didn't need anyone observing. He couldn't deny the attraction he felt to Jenna. Or that it wasn't one-sided. But whatever was happening between them would have to stay on the surface. Haylee would want to dig. "Don't make me take back my invitation."

Haylee smiled victoriously. "You wouldn't do that."

"Wanna bet?"

"What are you two bickering about?" Mom set her purse on the far kitchen counter and thumbed through the mail in her hands. Cody often left town before it was too chilly to leave the windows cracked, which would've alerted them to a car pulling into the driveway.

"Mom, would you like some quality time with your favorite granddaughter?" Haylee asked with extra sweetness in her tone. It was so ridiculous it almost always worked.

"I invited her to Warren's for halibut tacos."

"With *Jenna*." Haylee flashed an obnoxious smile.

"You don't want to be alone for your date?" Mom asked Cody. The complete innocence in her tone made Haylee laugh, which in turn made Melly giggle too. "What did I say?"

"It's not a date, Mom," Cody corrected. "Especially if I'm bringing my little sister as a chaperone."

"Sure seems like a date," Mom said.

Cody realized he wasn't about to win this debate, so he stopped contributing to it. "Jenna's supposed to text me when—" His phone buzzed on cue.

**Jenna:** I'm starving.
**Jenna:** Is this place dog-friendly?

Cody shot back a quick reply to let her know to

meet him in ten minutes and to warn him Haylee was tagging along. Warren's was only dog-friendly in warmer weather, but he suggested a walk along the bay after they ate to appease the bored pup.

**Jenna:** Oh good! I like Haylee.
**Jenna:** Is she bringing that super cute niece of yours too? :)

Cody couldn't fight the smile that tugged at his lips. Seemed Jenna meeting her favorite author—or perhaps her number-one fan—had finally warmed her up. Maybe now he could get a better read on her going forward.

"I mean, look at him, Mom. Is he not the definition of smitten right now?" Haylee teased. "Don't ask me why he's letting me crash the date, but it's *totally* a date. I'm just going for the free halibut tacos."

"Who said anything about free?" Cody teased after shooting a reply back to Jenna, promising that she could get in some Melly snuggles another time if she wanted.

"Cody," Mom said before they made it to the door. "Don't plan anything for Friday evening, okay?"

Though he put the pieces together earlier when Haylee and Sadie were using him as a middleman for their immature not-talking-to-each-other conversation, now he knew for certain. Mom was using his extra time in town to plan the going-away party he insisted he didn't want. "It's the Harvest Festival

Friday. I'm supposed to spend the whole day there with Jenna. It's number three on the list."

"You two can stop by after you're done at the festival."

Cody hurried out the door before he said something snide that Mom didn't deserve. She was one of the first to graciously accept he'd be gone for three whole years. That she'd only get to see her youngest son if she flew to him or something tragic happened. He could suck it up and act surprised to let her have one evening before he left.

"What's Jenna been doing all day anyway?" Haylee asked when she met him in his car. A car that would quickly become impractical if he really chose to stay in Alaska permanently, whether now or in three years. The decade-old Toyota Camry spent its winters in heated storage and had never seen a set of snow tires.

"Writing, I think."

"Wait, she's an author?"

"Yeah, she writes children's books. Illustrates them too."

"Just when I thought she couldn't get any cooler." She fiddled with her phone, typing some text or instant message with lighting quick fingers. "Her social media leaves a little bit of mystery, but what I do know is that she currently lives in Indiana and works in accounts receivable for some corporation." Haylee looked up from the screen. "That doesn't sound like Jenna, does it?"

Cody didn't exactly approve of his sister's snooping, but if the information was public, he supposed it was harmless. "I do have a hard time picturing her happy behind a desk," he admitted, omitting the nugget of knowledge he had about her belongings sitting in a trailer behind the lodge. She wasn't going back to the job.

"She doesn't have anything on here about her books. Wonder why that is."

*Bet it has something to do with that sister.* "Put a hold on the social media stalking, okay?" he said as he found a parking spot. "If you want to know more about her, you could try asking."

"Because that's working so well for you?"

"Are you hungry or not?"

"Starving."

"Then be a good sister and behave."

Haylee laughed all the way to the front door. "You invited me to crash a date. I'm not making any promises."

"Not a date." But Haylee had already slipped inside, his words lost to the music pouring out the open door.

# CHAPTER EIGHT

Jenna

"That was *Cody?*" Jenna asked in disbelief, still blown away by the list of movies she'd seen that he'd been in. She stole a glance at him from across the restaurant, allowing her gaze to linger a few seconds longer than necessary. *He really does look good in those jeans.* She never would've guessed he was the stuntman in any of them if Haylee hadn't told her. "I feel like we need a movie marathon or something. I want to rewatch all these."

"I think that's every movie he's been in," Haylee said, absently staring off in the distance as she thought about it. "Yep, that's all of them. Don't ask me about commercials, though. I've never been good at keeping track of those. He was much younger then anyway." She took a sip of soda. "And we can totally do a movie marathon. Might just be me and you if Cody does leave."

Jenna couldn't deny that her heart skipped a couple of beats at that comment. She glanced toward the bar to make sure Cody was still deep in conversation with the owner, Warren. "You think he might stay?"

"I think he *wants* to stay but doesn't fully realize it yet. Then there's that whole contract mess."

Though Jenna had spent the last twenty-four hours predominantly in her lodge room sketching her newest character and playing with the lyrical sentences for the first moose adventure book—aside from some short walks up to Lookout Point today to stretch Graham's legs and her aching muscles—she hadn't once stopped thinking about Cody.

She was falling for a man she hardly knew.

Maybe it was all this time the list required them to spend together.

Or maybe she was a sucker in the same way all his other adoring fans were.

But no matter the cause, Jenna couldn't stop the butterflies from joyfully tumbling around her belly at the sight of him even if she tried. She knew better than to believe he might stay, but she hoped for the impossible just the same.

"When's the last time your brother had a girl-friend?" Jenna dared to ask, despite the question showing her hand to someone who could be an ally just as easily as an enemy. Call it an instinct or a wish from her heart that they were sisters. She trusted Haylee.

"High school."

"You're kidding?"

Haylee slurped the last of her soda until the straw sucked air, then set the cup at the edge of the table. "Sadly, no. He says he dates while he's away, but I know my brother. He stays as far from serious as it gets. Or he has until you came along."

"I feel like you two are talking about me," Cody said, taking his seat at the round high top and setting a fresh plate of nachos in the middle. They'd finished their tacos an hour ago, but no one was in a hurry to leave. Unless the northern lights came out or Ed made an unexpected appearance, they were stalled on the list until they went kayaking tomorrow.

Cody looked back and forth suspiciously between the two women.

"Just talking about your movie star status," Haylee said, winking at Jenna when he wasn't paying attention. "We're doing a marathon next week so I can prove I'm not making up how many movies you've done stunts for. You're invited to join us." Haylee swiped a loaded nacho from the basket. "Oh, wait. You're going to be in *Maui*."

"We could do it sooner," Jenna heard herself say before she realized she'd been thinking the words.

"Sorry, ladies, you'll have to admire me from afar. My schedule is packed between this list, Mom's surprise going-away party I'm not supposed to know about, and packing up for the next three years."

Jenna's heart dropped at his nonchalant comment, crushing what little hope Haylee had ignited. It was foolish to think a stuntman as popular as Cody would give up a lifestyle he loved to stay in a small town for a woman he *just* met. That sort of thing only happened in romance novels. *Only in fiction.* Jenna nearly laughed out loud thinking if she possessed novel-writing abilities, she'd have another story to start penning tonight.

"I wish I could go with you guys tomorrow," Haylee said, oblivious to Jenna's suddenly dampened mood. "The last time I've been kayaking was before I was pregnant. But I promised Dad I'd help him with the booth for the festival."

"What booth?"

"Evans Outfitters does a booth every year at the Harvest Festival," Cody explained. "A lot of the local vendors have one. It drags the last of the tourists to town and reminds the residents to shop local when they're getting stocked up for a long winter ahead."

"Sometimes the road between here and Anchorage gets snowed in," Haylee added.

Jenna remembered traveling the two-lane highway to Sunset Ridge last week. There was only one route in and out for well over a hundred miles. "So, you get stuck here when that happens?"

Cody reached for another nacho, shaking off a black olive. Jenna smiled at the random thing they had in common. "We have pilots and bush planes in town for emergencies. It's not like we're completely cut off from the world. But it does stop any non-essential trips up north for a few days, sometimes a week or more until they get the road cleared."

"You talk about winter in Alaska like you remember what it's like," Haylee said with an eyeroll.

Jenna's phone buzzed in her pocket, and she silently cursed herself for bringing it. She'd hoped the hour she jumped online and handled some of the wedding tasks Whitney doled out would appease her sister, but she'd forgotten about the aftermath. Surely she'd screwed *something* up.

"Ex-boyfriend or something?" Haylee asked before she bit into a loaded nacho.

"I wish. An ex would be a cakewalk compared to my older sister." Jenna inhaled deeply as she flipped her phone from vibrate to silent. She'd given Whitney enough of her time for one day. It wasn't as though she'd hop on a plane and show up in Sunset Ridge because Jenna ignored her until morning. That required too much effort.

"Sounds like Sadie," Haylee murmured.

"No, she doesn't." Cody's stern tone seemed to catch both Haylee and Jenna off guard. "Sadie has things going on you know nothing about, Haylee," he added, his tone gentler but still firm enough to warn against further argument.

"I wouldn't know," Haylee said. "Not like she responds to me."

Sensing the sudden discomfort at the table, Jenna felt the urge to slip away. She had enough troublesome thoughts of her own to sort out without inviting more. "I'm sure Graham's getting anxious by now," she said, sliding her phone into her jacket pocket. "I better take him for that walk."

"I'll join you," Cody said so suddenly that a secret thrill raced through her. There was no list-related reason for him to come along. Which meant he *wanted* to spend time with her. Maybe there was a sliver of hope after all. "If you don't mind? I saved a nacho for Graham."

"Who am I to deny the dog a treat? Just don't give him one with cheese or I'm making him share a room with *you* tonight."

"You two are sickeningly adorable," Haylee said, a mischievous twinkle dancing in her eyes. "Don't stay out too late, now."

"You don't want to join us?" Jenna asked, pretending her heart wasn't racing at Haylee's comment. The more she allowed herself to enjoy this time spent with Cody, the more she risked a heartbreak she didn't want or need.

Haylee held up her phone. "Mom said Melly's asleep, which means I get to binge The Great British Bake Off in peace. Baby girl's been extra fussy these past few nights. Probably because she knows she won't see her uncle for *three* years." She slid off her stool and held out her hand for Cody's keys. "You don't mind giving him a ride home, do you, Jenna?"

"Not at all."

"Cool. Don't get into too much trouble, you two." With an obnoxious wink, Haylee hurried toward the door. Yes, Jenna *really* liked this sister.

"Wanna trade sisters?" she teased Cody as they made their way to the door. "I promise mine will *never* leave you alone."

"Whitney's older, I take it?" He waited by her truck as she clipped Graham's leash onto his collar and let him hop out. Cody held out his hand for a shake, but the pup did more of an intense high-five swipe since his attention was fixed on the nacho.

"Older by ten years." After Graham inhaled the massive nacho chip, the two headed toward the bay walk. "She was in college when my mom died. Had to drop out to take care of me. Grandpa was around too, but he was gone off and on at shoots. He'd just lost Grandma a couple years earlier, and well, we couldn't deny him the one thing that still brought him joy."

The last of the daylight sank into the horizon, causing the water to glisten. She tried to focus on the magical qualities, tucking that detail away for later use in a story. It was better than dwelling too heavily on a past she couldn't change.

"She resents the time she lost," Cody said thoughtfully, as if solving a puzzle.

"That's putting it mildly." Graham darted off the sidewalk, yanking her with him for a rustle in the fallen leaves. She planted her feet at the edge of the pavement and braced to keep him from getting away. "It might be a rabbit or a funny-looking tree branch. His reaction is always the same."

"Is that why you're moving to Alaska?" Cody asked, no judgment in his tone. Only curiosity that flattered her whether it was meant to or not. "To get away from your sister?"

Jenna couldn't remember the last time someone seemed so interested in her mundane life. She'd kept everything close to the vest for so many years. It felt good to trust someone again. Good, but also terrifying. Would they remain long-distance friends once he left?

"That's definitely a perk," she admitted. "But I'm not foolish enough to think Whitney would leave me alone just because I moved a few thousand miles away. Not unless I tossed my cell phone into the ocean for good."

"I imagine your editor wouldn't care for that."

"Not really."

Their hands grazed as they walked, causing Jenna's breath to hitch. The attraction between them was undeniable. But Jenna didn't want to be some woman Cody flirted with for only a few days. She widened the gap between them so the accidental brush wouldn't happen again. He'd have his pick of women in Maui, and she'd be nothing more than a forgotten memory.

"Did I tell you Whitney's getting married?" Jenna said to draw attention away from the physical contact that was still making her hand tingle minutes later.

"When?"

"In two months." Jenna didn't have to feel buzzing in her pocket to sense the incoming text messages. Or maybe Whitney had switched to calling since she was likely off work now. Either way, she wasn't answering tonight. "I'm not going." She expected him to ask why or tell her that was an extreme decision she might later regret. But when Cody said nothing, she went on. "The guy she's marrying is a jerk, to put it lightly. She's settling for good looks and money. She cares more about what other people think than her own long-term happiness. If I ever get married, it'll be for love."

"*If?*"

Jenna shrugged, though Cody probably didn't notice in the darkness between light poles. "Grandpa used to tell me stories about how he met Grandma. How he knew she was the one the moment he laid eyes on her. How every day they spent together confirmed they were soulmates. He never remarried, you know." The night chill disappeared as the warmth of those memories filled her. "I promised myself a long time ago that I wouldn't settle down unless I found what they had."

Cody's silence made her heart pound. She hoped

he hadn't read into what she said the wrong way. He was attractive, certainly. But she already knew he wasn't marriage material.

"Anyway, the guy Whitney's marrying . . ." She let out a defeated sigh. "He made a pass at me during their engagement party."

"You're kidding?"

"You're the only person I've told. Other than my sister." Jenna stopped while Graham watered a tree with enthusiasm. "She didn't believe me, of course. That's when I decided I didn't want to go to the wedding. Also the same point in time she decided I didn't need to live in her basement anymore." Jenna typed up her two-week notice that night after her tossing and turning made it impossible to sleep.

"Why do you let her treat you the way she does?" Cody asked as they arrived at the junction to the pier. Graham made a hard left, insisting they travel down it. "You are allowed to cut toxic people out of your life, even if they're family."

"Aside from raising me after my mom died, Whitney let me live with her rent-free for two years while I attended a special school for illustrating. While I was attending, I made a connection that later landed me my first publishing deal." Jenna slowed as they reached the end of the deserted pier. The chilly ocean breeze cut right through her jacket, so she folded her arms tighter around her chest. "Had I been working full time during that school, well, let's just say I wouldn't have been able to juggle all that.

I'm grateful for what she did for me. It allowed me to fulfill a lifelong dream."

"You're cold." Cody stood beside her in the perfect spot to block the worst of the wind. It was a sweet gesture, though what she really craved was his arm around her, hugging him against his warm chest.

Graham let out a bark when something jumped in the water just off the pier. She focused on his pointed ears because it kept her from gazing into Cody's eyes. Had she ever yearned for someone to gather her into their arms and kiss her *this* much before?

"Are those—" She pointed to the dark sky, where she swore she saw a swish of green. Cody watched with her for several moments, but if the northern lights had made an appearance earlier, they weren't eager to return.

"Number four waits for another night," Cody said, lifting one corner of his mouth in a half smile that activated the butterflies every time. Her gaze dropped to his lips and she found it nearly impossible to look away.

"Maybe we should head back," Jenna said to save herself from making a foolish move she couldn't take back. They still had seven list items to complete, and she didn't want to make things awkward between them.

Cody slipped both hands into his sweatshirt pockets as they turned toward shore. "When are you going to tell your sister you're not going back?"

"I could tell her right now and she wouldn't

believe me." Jenna shook her head at the impossibility of telling her sister anything she actually listened to. "She didn't believe I was driving to Alaska until she saw my name on the PTO calendar at work. She tried to talk me out of it, of course. Thinks that coming here so soon after Grandpa died isn't healthy."

"She wasn't as close with him as you were, was she?" he guessed as they reached the sidewalk and turned back toward the truck.

"No." Jenna hadn't talked to anyone this honestly about her sister . . . ever. Not even Grandpa when he was alive because she didn't want to put him in the middle. It felt therapeutic to get everything off her chest, but she realized how it all sounded. "I love my sister. I just don't necessarily . . ."

"Like her?"

"Does that make me a terrible person?" She laughed to lighten the heavy moment, but her heart raced in anticipation of his answer. She'd stopped letting opinions of others affect her a long time ago, but suddenly Cody's opinion mattered a whole lot.

"No, it doesn't."

Relief flooded her body at his words. "Really?"

"I think it makes you an incredibly mature woman. Sadie could take a few lessons from you." Cody scrubbed a hand over his face, messing up his windblown hair in a way that made Jenna want to fix it. Or maybe she really just wanted to run her fingers through his disheveled blond hair. "Your happiness or worth shouldn't come from your sister. And it shouldn't be robbed because of her, either."

His profound words resonated in her soul. "Wow, you're good at this advice thing, aren't you?"

"So I've been told."

Too soon they were standing beside her truck, the night about to come to a close. She wished for an excuse to prolong the evening, especially knowing they only had a few more days to spend together. A lot could happen in three years, and it was entirely possible they might part ways and never see each other again. "I guess I'll see you tomorrow?"

"Be ready bright and early," he said.

"Haylee doesn't mind watching Graham?"

"The only reason Haylee doesn't have a dog is because Mom and Dad won't allow it. You should be more worried about her kidnapping Graham than him being a nuisance." Cody reached out toward her cheek, his fingertips grazing her skin.

*Is he really going to kiss me?*

Her breath stalled in her lungs as she dared only to stare at his Kenai Peninsula sweatshirt.

"You had a hair," he said, tucking it beneath her ear and dropping his hand. Leaving Jenna to feel incredibly foolish for allowing impossible fantasies to take hold and rob her of her good sense.

"Right." She cleared her throat and stepped back to open the door. "So, see you tomorrow?"

"Are you going to make me walk home?" he teased, his tone easygoing and effortless.

"Right. You need a ride." She hoped the darkness hid her reddening cheeks, but she turned away just in case. If Cody was feeling even half of what she was in that moment, nothing about his voice or expression gave him away. Leave it to Jenna to fall for a man who would never see her as more than a friend.

# CHAPTER NINE

CODY

"Want to sit up front?" Cody offered Jenna as Liam Davies finished the preflight checks on the outside of his Super Cub. They couldn't have asked for a more beautiful day this late in the season. Because most tourist places had closed up shop for the winter, they might even get lucky enough to have the lake to themselves.

Lips pinched tightly together, Jenna shook her head. Her sunglasses hid her eyes, making it hard to get an accurate read on her. Something he was still having enough trouble doing without obstacles. Was she nervous about flying or about being in the water? Or was it the prospect of seeing a bear—which they likely would—that unsettled her?

"The view's amazing from any window, but it's the best from the copilot seat."

"Back is fine."

"Ready to go?" Liam called from the opposite side of the plane.

"Jenna?"

She crawled into the back seat of the plane without another word, shaky hands struggling with her seat belt until it finally clicked into place. She sat rigidly, her hands tucked between her legs. He could sense her nervousness like a thick fog in the air. *Afraid of flying it is.*

"I'll sit in back with Jenna," Cody told Liam.

Liam smirked, but at least he had the decency to keep his thoughts to himself. Cody didn't want to give Jenna the wrong impression, but he wasn't so heartless that he'd make her face this fear alone. He'd met a few women who faked fears to get his attention; Jenna definitely wasn't one of them. Until this very moment, he wasn't certain she *had* any fears.

"What are you doing?" Jenna snapped when he crawled into the cramped seat beside her and buckled in.

"Riding back here with you."

"Why?"

Admittedly, he missed the easygoing Jenna with lowered walls from last night. He'd almost kissed her —twice. Once on the pier when he noticed her shivering, and again at the truck when he made an excuse about tucking a stray strand of hair behind her ear.

114

That version of Jenna had nearly let him. But kissing her would do neither of them any good when it came time to saying goodbye.

There was no threat of kissing now. Not with those walls fortified back in place. Why did he so badly want to shake that up?

"Do I need a reason?" he finally answered because he felt Jenna's glacial stare through her sunglasses penetrating his comfort zone. She had an effect on him no one else did, and he wasn't certain what to make of it. It was easier now to pick it apart. In a few days, it wouldn't matter anyway. *Right?*

"You feel sorry for me." She groaned, turning her head over her shoulder to peer out the window as Liam fired up the engine.

"You never mentioned you were afraid of flying."

"You didn't ask."

He dared to set a compassionate hand above her knee, resting it gently in hopes she'd relax from his touch and not tense up even more. Or worse, toss it away. "If there was another way to get to this place without taking a plane, we would. But even by boat it would take too long."

"And we don't have that kind of time. Yeah, so you've reminded me." Though some of her coolness today was definitely a direct result of her fear, Cody wondered if there was more. Maybe she panicked when she realized her walls had dropped too much, and in turn, reinforced them twice as much.

It should bring him relief.

He took his hand from her knee and folded it with his other in his lap to keep it from misbehaving. If Jenna wasn't falling for him, it would be easier to leave. Nothing to feel guilty about. Nothing for Eddie Kingsley to haunt him about.

Except, Cody suspected he was falling for Jenna, too.

Or maybe already had.

She gripped his knee, digging her fingers in when the plane lifted into the air. It didn't matter that her nails threatened to draw blood. Her touch still sent his pulse racing. Maybe it was because she so rarely reached for him, or that uninvited feelings had taken deeper root than he suspected. Yeah, he was definitely falling for her, too. *What a mess*.

"Look," he said, pointing out the window, thankful for the beautiful sunny day and the soaring wings of an eagle to distract them. The wildlife didn't mind the chill, but it was certainly easier to spot them without gloomy drizzle and fog. "There's an eagle."

"Really?" Jenna stiffly leaned forward an inch, accepting the hand he offered and giving it a death-grip squeeze. He wondered if she'd clam up this same way tomorrow when he surprised her with a library visit. He'd already reached out to the head librarian Fiona James to sign Jenna up for story hour. She'd rearranged the library's entire schedule to accommodate a *real live* children's author tomorrow at nine thirty.

"See it?"

"Oh, yeah!" Her grip relaxed enough to allow blood flow in his hand again. He didn't mind that she held on, despite how problematic that was proving to be for both of them. He ignored the warning voices whispering to him and instead fixed his attention out the window.

"One down, at least eight more to go if we want to beat your grandpa's record."

"How are we supposed to take selfies with nine or more eagles?" Jenna asked, her gaze fixed out her window.

"Hopefully Jenkins will settle for one." Because Cody didn't know, either.

"Look, there's another one!" She lifted her sunglasses, setting them on top of her head, revealing the sparkle of excitement in her brown eyes so dark they were nearly black. Except this close up, he could identify a handful of golden flecks in her irises.

Cody forced himself to peer out his own window before he *did* kiss her.

"I knew Alaska would be beautiful, but I— Just wow!" He wasn't certain whether it was their joined hands that broke through her icy layer this morning or the list-related distraction, but he much preferred this warmer version of Jenna. "You're really going to up and leave for *three* years." She shook her head. "You're crazy. This place is magical."

"You haven't gone through a winter yet," Cody said, purposely leaning in because the engine made it hard to hear one another without almost yelling. Sitting closer to Jenna was an added bonus. Or so he told himself. "I could come back in three years and find you packed up and left two days after the first major snowfall."

"I think you underestimate me. I'm from the Midwest. We have plenty of snow. It's Graham's favorite time—" Her easy smile vanished in an instant when the plane dipped forward. Her grip went from comfortable to cutting off the circulation in his hand in a single lost heartbeat.

"Liam's getting ready to land," Cody said, tempted to drape an arm over her shoulders and pull her tight against him because he knew she'd let him in this moment of vulnerability. Would it be so ludicrous to stay in Sunset Ridge and see where this might go? It'd been a decade since he last left his heart open for the taking. Something he swore he'd never do again after it was so easily crushed. But something about Jenna and the way he felt in her presence made him flirt with the temptation to try again.

Never mind that his entire career—one that he loved—was riding on his showtime Monday morning.

Yeah, he was definitely in trouble.

Jenna squeezed her eyes shut as they descended, not opening them again until the plane stopped rolling forward. She loosened her death-grip one finger at a time.

"We can't walk back to Sunset Ridge later?" she asked through a pitiful laugh.

"We could, but I'd definitely miss my flight."

"I'm not sure I'd mind that."

Cody stroked the side of her hand with his thumb, unable and unwilling to keep his gaze from dropping to her soft lips. He could deny his feelings all he wanted, but he couldn't keep lying to himself by pretending he hadn't thought about kissing her nearly every minute since they first met.

The back door popped open, and Jenna yanked her hand free of Cody's as if it were on fire.

Never before had Cody been so annoyed to have a moment shattered. He'd always chalked up missed kisses to fate. These serendipitous interruptions often saved him from breaking hearts, and he welcomed them. Until now.

He exited from the back and stepped onto solid ground. He focused his attention to the sky, hoping another eagle would soar by and distract them both from what nearly transpired in the plane with a witness. In a tandem kayak, she wouldn't be within kissing distance.

"I'll see you two in four hours," Liam said once the kayaks and equipment were unloaded.

"Thanks for the ride," Cody said, shaking his hand.

"Tessa would've killed me if I said no." Liam looked at Jenna. "My wife really likes you. Between you and me, I think she's buttering you up to get some autographs tom—"

"Thanks, Liam," Cody interrupted before Liam

could spill the beans about a story hour that obviously wasn't limited to the second grade class anymore. She'd murder him in his sleep if half the town showed up to the library. He glanced up at the sky, hoping Eddie was watching them. He'd be chuckling for sure, that same sparkle dancing in his eyes that Jenna was starting to share more and more.

Jenna yanked on Cody's jacket sleeve as Liam hopped into his plane. "*Four* hours?"

"It's a good hour on the water before we'll see Bear Glacier." Mom had also sent along a lunch—a brilliant idea if ever there was one—after admitting how much she liked Jenna . . . and asking about the *date* that wasn't a date three times. Haylee had given plenty of details to appease her when Cody kept his lips sealed.

"An hour? Maybe I should've spent more time in the gym like Whitney insisted," Jenna muttered, her voice nearly drowned out by Liam taking off.

Cody cupped both of her elbows, admiring how adorable she looked in that fuzzy white ear warmer, and waited until she met his gaze. "I promise there's no cell reception out here. Let's leave our annoying siblings at home where they belong and enjoy this rare, gorgeous fall day, okay?"

As Liam flew away, an eagle cried out overhead. Together they said, "Three!"

Fishing his phone from an interior jacket pocket, he put an arm around Jenna and guided them in line with the eagle soaring above them. He snapped a dozen or more photos, hopeful *one* would satisfy Eddie's terms.

"Let me see," Jenna said, leaning closer as she scrolled through their attempts.

"We might have to keep trying if we see more."

"This one's only a little blurry." He stopped on the photo she favored, more focused on the dazzling smile he'd captured than the fuzzy bird that could as easily pass for a hawk as an eagle. But he wouldn't dare delete this one.

"I think it's a good one."

Their gaze met, and Cody's traitorous eyes dropped right to those soft lips. This time, he didn't fight it. Couldn't fight it. He cupped her cheek with his free hand, stroking her chilled skin with his thumb. Their gazes locked, and for once, no words were spoken. He stalled several seconds, allowing her every opportunity to pull away as he ever so slowly leaned in.

Their lips an inch apart, Jenna reached for his neck and yanked him the rest of the way down. The kiss ignited a series of fireworks around them. Cody dropped his phone into his coat pocket and wrapped his arm around her, pulling her closer. Her cinnamon-vanilla scent invaded his senses, but he welcomed it in because it felt like . . . *home*.

Breathless. That's how Cody felt when their lips finally broke apart. Breathless and slightly dizzy at the exhilarating moment. He suspected kissing Jenna would be nice, but this . . . this was on a level all its own.

Before he could search Jenna's eyes for what she might be feeling, she wriggled free and headed toward the kayak, sending him an easy smile over her shoulder. "You going to show me how to use this thing or what?"

A mixture of disappointment and contentment warred inside him. They both knew this could never go anywhere, but at least she wasn't vocalizing immediate regret. Eddie might haunt him for it, but Cody'd never regret that kiss. He'd carry it with him to Maui and whatever came next. "You ever gone kayaking before?"

"Nope. Probably why it's on the list."

Of the thirteen items Eddie included on his bucket list, this one most appealed to Cody. Nothing he loved more than getting into nature and just *being*. He craved it more than any adrenaline rush or social gathering with new friends. The older he got, the more he realized he appreciated the silence above all. "You're in for a real treat, then."

She spun in a slow circle, taking in their surroundings. The snowcapped mountains, the still crystal-blue water reflecting both the open sky and nearby icebergs, and the rocky shore. "I wish I'd come sooner," she said, her smile both awe-inspired and a bit sad. "Grandpa tried to get me to visit last summer, but I—"

"Nothing you can do to change the past," he said,

helping her into the front of the kayak. She'd slipped on a pair of gloves, but he felt the heat of her touch nonetheless. "But the future is for the taking."

"Pretty heavy insight for a man whose next three years are spoken for," Jenna said, a raised eyebrow daring him to challenge her statement.

"It's a future I chose."

"Why, exactly?" she asked, accepting the paddle he handed her once she was situated.

"My agent said it would open doors for me in the future. That if I do this show and stick out the full three years, I'll be able to handpick my work." He left out the small fortune the show promised to pay him each year. He didn't need the money, but it was a nice financial cushion for whatever came next. "I have a list of places I've never traveled. This might be my opportunity to see some of those places."

"Such as?"

He pushed them into the water before securing himself in the back. "Greece, for one."

"Now, there's a place I'd love to see. But unless they invent teleporting, I don't think I'll ever make it."

He pushed off fully from the shallow water and together they found sync in their paddling efforts. "You did just fine on the flight out here."

"It was all of twenty minutes. I think it takes longer to fly over an entire ocean." She shook her head, her black ponytail bouncing back and forth with the movement. He rather liked the sight of

Jenna sharing a tandem kayak with him. Wondered what it might be like to *still* share moments like this years from now. One kiss would never be enough. He was lying to himself if he thought it would be. But the situation was more complicated than simply choosing whether or not to stay. "You want to know what I think?"

"What?"

"You're running away."

"Is that what Haylee told you?"

"Actually, no." Jenna glanced at him over his shoulder, but with those pesky sunglasses covering her eyes again, he was left to wonder what lingered in her gaze. "I mean, she told me you haven't had a serious girlfriend since high school. That helped me put some of the pieces together."

Cody felt uncomfortably vulnerable. He was the expert at reading people. Very few were ever able to figure him out. Eddie had been an exception, and the old man had suggested the same as his granddaughter was now. At least he understood where Jenna got her insightfulness. "I like my lifestyle," he countered, only his tone nonchalant. His erratic pulse was anything but. "It's a lot to ask of someone, to put up with me constantly leaving. Or taking a last-minute assignment and bouncing from one spot to another." One winter season, he'd ping-ponged between three different movie sets, sometimes boarding a plane every few days.

"Not if she came with you," Jenna pointed out.

He stared at her, watching the breeze lift individual strands of her ponytail. Relieved she wasn't so easily able to study him from where she sat. With her fear of flying, he doubted she'd ever be that person. Too much to hope that was what she was suggesting. Plus, there was Graham. She'd peppered the pup with hugs and kisses and left Haylee with a tote bag worth of treats, all for a half-day trip.

"Not many women are up for that."

"Sure, they are." Jenna pointed at another eagle in the sky. "That makes four!"

"Only five more to go." Part of him hoped they wouldn't see enough eagles to mark that off his list. Or that Ed would remain elusive and give him a reason to stay. But it was wishful thinking at best. Not showing up to Maui would have irreversible consequences. *So does leaving.*

"You're running," Jenna said matter-of-factly.

"Running from what?"

"Any chance of commitment or falling in love." She lifted her sunglasses to her forehead when she turned back. "Who was she?"

"Who was who?"

"The high school sweetheart who broke your heart?"

"I'm not the only one keeping an arm's length where relationships are concerned," he said, eager to dodge that conversation. He was only seventeen back then. He'd grown a lot. Learned a lot. He was an entirely different person now. "What about you?"

"What about me?"

"No boyfriend back home?"

"It's not for lack of effort, believe me," Jenna said seriously. "I'm picky. I know what I'm looking for, and if it's unrealistic, then I'm okay being alone. As long as I have a dog and my art can bring me joy again, I know I'd be content."

Content felt like settling, but Cody didn't say that out loud when he was doing the same thing. He was content traveling and being a stuntman. He enjoyed trying new things and chasing the adrenaline rush those stunts provided. He liked meeting new people and absorbing their stories. But it all left him feeling merely *content*.

"Oh, my— Cody, there's a bear." She looked at him, her expression a mixture of shock and terror. "What do we do?"

"Relax," he said. "She's far enough away she won't bother us as long as we leave her and her cubs to fish."

"Cubs?" Jenna's tone perked as she searched the shore for the two bear cubs he'd already spotted emerging from the brush. "You know, I never suspected Bear Glacier kayaking would include actual bears. Just figured it was the name of the glacier." She dug into her interior jacket pocket and pulled out her phone. "Think you can turn the kayak so we can get a picture that doesn't upset mama bear?"

"On it." Cody felt relieved for the much-needed topic shift. If he could, he'd personally thank the grizzly for saving him from an embarrassing line of questions about his younger self and what he may or may not be running from. But that earlier earth-shattering kiss . . . that was something he couldn't so easily forget.

# CHAPTER TEN

Jenna

"I'm not coming back to Indiana, Whitney." Jenna paced in her lodge room, wishing despite its cozy spaciousness, that it was larger. Graham was curled on the bed as to keep out of her path. She'd been going around with her sister for the past twenty minutes, and *still* Whitney didn't seem to hear her. *Some things never change.*

"Did you get everything for the centerpieces ordered like I asked you a dozen times?" Typical Whitney, ignoring anything she didn't want to hear and making the conversation all about her. The more distance Jenna got from her sister, the clearer some things became about their fractured relationship.

"No." It felt oddly satisfying to give her the answer.

"What do you mean *no?*"

"Whitney, your fiancé *hit* on me. Does that not bother you?" She'd kept her lips sealed about the incident after Whitney chewed her out the first time, claiming Jenna was jealous and desperate for attention. Getting kicked out of Whitney's basement with virtually no notice was supposed to be some kind of warning from her sister to keep her mouth shut *or else*. But enough was enough. She was done staying silent or being pushed around. "During your engagement party, no less."

"You're still telling yourself that lie?"

"It's not a lie. He tried to *kiss* me." The memory of him cornering her away from everyone still gave her the heebie jeebies. A kiss wasn't all he was after, either. It was only her quick thinking that saved her.

"That's not what he told me. Said you kicked him in the shin when he turned you down."

Jenna let out a long groan. "Of course you believe him over your own flesh and blood."

"He's the one telling the truth."

Jenna's heart squeezed. For years, she'd wished she could figure out what made Whitney the way she was. She'd been searching memories from her childhood, before their mom passed, and couldn't remember if that event changed her sister or if she'd always been this way. *More like Mom.* "Do you remember when Mom and Charmane got into that huge fight?"

"Who?"

"Charmane. Mom's *best* friend." The more she'd been opening up lately, the more she remembered from her younger years. Memories that were slowly filling in blanks she'd had for years. "They had a big fight about Mom's boyfriend, Chuck."

"Why are you bringing *him* up?" Whitney was seconds from hanging up the phone, and maybe Jenna should let her. But she felt a duty as her sister to make one last effort to get through. If Whitney still didn't want to listen, then Jenna would stick to loving her from afar.

"He made a pass at Charmane. At Christmas."

"No, he didn't. *She* made one at him under the mistletoe. She'd been planning it for weeks. That's what Chuck—" Whitney gasped. "How long have you been planning to seduce *my* fiancé?"

Well, this was going nowhere fast. Jenna groaned, realizing when her sister went silent that she hadn't made that sound only in her mind. *Oops.* "Look, I'm not coming back to Indiana, Whitney. It has very little to do with your rotten fiancé, either. If you want to lie to yourself about the womanizer with a fat bank account you're about to marry, I'm done trying to talk sense into you. I'm staying in Alaska for *me*. Because that's what I want."

"You have *some* nerve," Whitney growled. It was a good thing her sister was thousands of miles away and unable to leap through the phone. "After everything I've done for you! Are you going to pay me back for all those months I let you stay with me for *free*? All that time I fed you and let you hibernate in the basement so you could work on your stupid art?"

Jenna's heart squeezed painfully at that last comment. "Stupid art." She repeated the words so softly she barely heard them leave her quivering lips. Whitney continued her tirade, but Jenna disconnected the call without listening.

Tears streamed silently down her cheeks. A sleepy Graham quickly came to her rescue, crawling into her lap when she dropped back onto the bed. She hugged him tight, and the wonderful fur-child let her squeeze him for all he was worth. "It's not fair, Graham Cracker. I keep trying to save this relationship. Why am I the only one who cares?"

He licked her hand twice, then her cheek.

"You are the best thing that's ever happened to me," she said into his fur. "Better than any work promotion or publishing contract. Better than—" The memory of that spine-tingling kiss momentarily erased everything that was going wrong in her life. How many times had Cody's lips ended up dangerously close to hers these past two days until she finally yanked him that final inch? Did she have any regrets? Absolutely not. "Okay, you and that kiss are kind of tied for first at the moment. It was a *really* great kiss."

A knock at the door drew her attention to the alarm clock beside her bed. Cody promised to pick up her at nine, but didn't elaborate on their plans. Before Whitney called and ruined her morning, she'd spent it wondering what list item they'd do next. Willamina's Big Dipper wasn't open until lunchtime. The northern lights weren't visible during the day. And the Harvest Festival was still a day away. "Maybe we're hunting for Ed."

Graham groaned his disapproval, which made her finally laugh and wipe her cheeks clean of tears. "Not *hunt*-hunting him. We need his picture is all." A quick peek in the mirror confirmed her waterproof mascara had done its job.

The dog beat her to the door after another knock sounded. She opened it and asked, "Are we searching for Ed today?"

Cody's gaze traveled up and down once. Jenna felt a flutter in her tummy, wondering if he might kiss her again. Yes, she'd spent an inordinate amount of time on her makeup—her hair was a lost cause outside of a ponytail. Maybe she'd tried on three different outfits before settling on a pair of dark skinny jeans and the burnt-orange top she'd frivolously purchased at the Forget Me Not earlier that week.

Graham barged his way between them, leaning against Cody's legs until he crouched to pet him.

"Ed has been spotted around town, but not since yesterday when he was sneaking blueberries from Tillie Grant's kitchen window. Odds are iffy today. Ready to go?" he asked, still Graham's prisoner on the floor. "Yes, you too, Graham Cracker."

"How did you know—"

Cody reached for the dog's leash on a nearby chair

and clipped it onto Graham's collar before standing. "Know what?"

"That his real name is Graham Cracker?" The only other person who knew that was Grandpa, and he'd been sworn to secrecy to keep Whitney from ruining that particular joy.

"I didn't."

She slipped on a jacket and grabbed her purse, wondering if Grandpa had shared her secret with Cody during one of those visits to Alaska. She was curious how much he might've talked about her, but didn't feel right asking. "I named him after the very first character I ever created," Jenna admitted as she locked the door behind her. "I was four."

"Was it a dog?" Cody guessed.

"A cat, actually. Mom used to sneak scraps to a stray when she didn't think I was watching. Claimed she didn't want us girls to get attached. But the cat naturally turned tame since we were *both* sneaking him food."

"Cody Evans? I thought you'd gotten on a plane by now," Cadence, one of the three Whitmore sisters who owned and managed the lodge, said as they stepped into the lobby. She stood beside the buffet, refilling K-cups, creamer packets, and utensils. The aroma of freshly baked muffins—banana-nut Jenna knew because she'd already swiped one—danced around them.

"Leaving on Saturday," he said, the words a blunt reminder that he was a temporary part of her life, amazing kiss or not. Sunset Ridge would certainly feel like a different place without her personal tour guide. Which made her all the more determined to steal one more kiss before he left. A good-bye kiss she could remember him by.

"Maui this time?"

"Yep, that's the gig."

"I've only been to Hawaii once, when my niece was first born. But I hear Maui is a favorite of those who've island hopped." Cadence opened another box of K-cups, its beautiful packaging tempting Jenna to reconsider her dislike of coffee. That caramel-toffee flavor looked delicious.

"Maui's nice," Cody said, his words so generic they gave Jenna pause.

"Jenna, is everything going all right for you?"

"For me?"

"With your room?"

She felt a tinge of embarrassment at the misunderstanding, but recovered quickly enough. "Oh yes, it's wonderful. I should be checking out by Saturday." *Or taking up permanent residence for three years until Cody comes back to finish the list.* Either way, she'd decided to become an Alaskan resident. "Is that a problem? I know there's a festival this weekend—"

"It's no issue at all. Things start to slow down around here this time of year, even for this final festival. We've got two empty rooms if anyone shows up last-minute."

Cody pulled at his phone, glancing at the screen. "We better head out. Don't want to be late."

"Late?"

"Enjoy Maui if I don't see you before you leave," Cadence called after them, the conversation leaving Jenna with a pit in her stomach.

When Cody first announced he was delaying his flight, she didn't have the good sense to appreciate the extra time they'd get to spend together. Now that it was coming so quickly to a close, emotions stirred inside her she didn't want to feel. A kiss or two was harmless enough. But feelings were quite another thing.

"How are you with surprises?" Cody asked as he stole her truck keys from her palm and hopped into the driver's side after Graham.

"Not great." Cody cranked the engine before she took a step closer, rolling down the back window halfway for Graham. "Cody!"

"C'mon, there's no time."

"Ugh!" She marched around to the passenger side, wanting to be mad at him. But she was much too touched by the way he was acting with her dog this morning to be more than mildly annoyed. "Where are we going?"

"If I tell you, it won't be a surprise, then, will it?"

"Is this on the list?"

"You're not getting any hints from me."

Jenna folded her arms over her chest, well aware she was acting like a pouty child. "Fine." But secretly, she felt a slice of excitement. What if he was taking her somewhere romantic? Preferably somewhere that didn't require an airplane ride to get to. Maybe she'd never gotten seriously involved with a man, but she still recognized when one was interested. And even if Cody was in the habit of running from anything serious, he most definitely was interested. No man kissed the way he did if he weren't.

"What is this?" she asked when he pulled into a parking spot a block off the downtown strip.

"C'mon. They're expecting you." Cody and Graham hopped out of the truck and started walking down the sidewalk toward a two-story brick building, leaving Jenna sitting in the truck. She'd seen buildings like that before. She didn't need to read the sign to know where they were.

"Why can't I ever have a *good* surprise?" she grumbled, reluctantly following the duo. Dozens of cars were parked along both sides of the street. A school bus sat off to the side. How many people were inside? If she'd only talked to the lawyer about a loophole instead of barricading herself in a lodge room to write or allowing Cody to whisk her away to places without cell reception, maybe she'd have gotten a pass for this one item.

"I didn't tell Fiona which book you wanted to read," Cody said, stopping and waiting for her to catch up. He offered his arm, most likely to keep her from running off. But he had her dog. She wasn't going anywhere without Graham, even into hiding to avoid public speaking.

Jenna had turned down multiple requests to read her books in front of an audience. She loved kids and appreciated that they devoured her stories. She loved what libraries did for young readers. But she fit so easily into an introverted role in accounts receivable because it didn't require her to get up in front of anyone. Her palms were sweaty and she hadn't even seen the inside of the library. There might be a hundred people packed inside or maybe just one. Her panic was the same.

"Oh, you made it!" a woman in a long, flowing skirt decorated with sprinkles of sequins greeted. "I'm Fiona James, head librarian." Jenna offered her a weak smile that somehow resulted in Fiona clasping one of Jenna's hands in both of hers. "We're so excited to have you for story hour. We rarely get a celebrity in town. We do have Denver Grant, but his murder mysteries aren't quite appropriate for second graders."

Cody followed behind as Jenna was pulled into the open area of the library. Bookshelves lined the walls and were displayed across the floor in diagonal patterns. Jenna heard the chatter of a crowd before she spotted the mob in the back of the room where the bookshelves tapered off.

"We have an event room, but we got a slightly bigger turnout than expected."

Jenna whipped her head over shoulder, pointing a narrowed glare at Cody. Dropping by unannounced for a surprise reading at story hour would've been challenging enough for her anxiety. But now that half the town was crammed into the back of the library, it felt like an impossible feat. She'd likely freeze up there in front of all those people and die of mortification.

"If I survive this," she said through gritted teeth, "I'm going to kill you."

"I'm just following the list." His nonchalant tone really grated on her nerves in moments like this one. If Cody ended up staying—which Jenna knew was a one-percent chance at best—they might end up driving each other mad.

Graham looked up at her from Cody's side, offering her encouragement with his big brown doe eyes and wagging tail. He thought Jenna's celebrity status was exciting. She scratched him behind the ears, mostly to calm her nerves. Partially to stand a little closer to Cody. Too close and she might actually strangle him.

"Cody didn't tell me what book you wanted to read, so I pulled every one we had on the shelf." Fiona pointed toward a table beside a podium. "Some are checked out, but we have most of them right now."

For the briefest of moments, Jenna wished she'd dug into her trailer and pulled out the couple boxes of books she'd packed. But the idea of sitting through an in-person signing was more terrifying than reading one of her books out loud. She only kept the personal stash to mail signed copies to fans she never had to meet in person. "I'll pick one of those," she said because Fiona was looking at her expectantly.

"How about *I* pick one?" Cody suggested, not the least bit bothered by the gathering crowd, even with the handful of waves he got from the audience. Jenna had never lived in a town small enough to be recognized by so many people. It would take some getting used to.

Cody sifted through the pile and handed one over, but Jenna was too nervous to even glimpse the title.

"Attention, everyone," Fiona's voice squeaked through the microphone. She made a couple of adjustments and spoke again without the feedback. "We're so thrilled to have such a huge turnout for story hour. We don't want to keep you waiting, so without further ado, let me introduce J.A. Kingsley." As the crowd clapped, Fiona looked back at Jenna. "You'll have to forgive me. All I know about you I found on your website." She looked back at her podium and adjusted a pair of reading glasses. "J.A Kingsley is the author of more than twenty-five picture books. She writes *and* illustrates all her own titles."

Jenna could recite her bio by memory. Her website, provided by her publisher, was one of the few places she could loiter and feel good without Whitney crushing her spirit about it. She'd discovered early in her publishing career that sharing her accomplishments on social media did nothing more than make her an open target where her sister and their work friends were concerned. None of them took seriously what Jenna did *on the side*.

*They were never friends at all.*

All too soon, a hush fell over the room. Dozens of young eyes gathered on the carpet in front of the rows of chairs stared up at her expectantly. She didn't even see which book she grabbed before she dropped into her chair, her hands shakier than ever.

Cody and Graham sat off to the side, both their zealous smiles calming her rattled nerves. Jenna felt a sense of calm wash over her, as if the duo were somehow sending her the steadying energy she needed. She remembered Grandpa describing a scenario just like this one, where he was forced to confront a fear and Grandma helped him through it with no more than an encouraging smile from the sidelines.

With a deep breath, Jenna held up the book and smiled at the eager crowd as she opened it.

## CHAPTER ELEVEN

Cody

"Is this not the best caribou chili you've ever had?" Cody asked, moaning in delight between spoonfuls. He'd definitely miss Willamina's specialty soups over the next three years. He wondered if he could lay on the charm thick enough to get her to send him some.

"Considering I've never *tried* caribou until this moment, it's the best one I've had, yes." Jenna sprinkled a few soup crackers along the top, as she'd done a few bites ago. "What?" she asked when she caught him staring. "I like my crackers to crunch with every bite."

Cody's gaze lingered longer than he should let it, but he wasn't thinking so clearly anymore. Not after yesterday's kiss that still buzzed on his lips or watching Jenna crush that story hour. He had no idea she had such stage fright, but once she got into her element, she was dynamite. It was incredibly attractive to watch her come alive and share her passion with so many eager faces, young and old alike. Which was why he pulled out the folded paper from his pocket. His eyes needed something to distract them besides the stunning woman in the booth across from him before he did something rash like slide in beside her and steal another kiss for half the town to witness. "We only have three things left."

"We've really done ten already?"

"Do you remember the first day, how you dreaded spending time with me?" He was sure to add an extra cheesy edge to his tone because it always made her smile wider.

She let out a soft, easy laugh. "You mean the day I caught you trespassing?"

"Well, there was that." He recalled how inconvenient this whole bucket list business felt when it'd caught him off guard. He'd agreed to it for Eddie's sake—and Jenna's. But he wondered if the old man realized that Cody needed it, too. Or if he'd get a good chuckle to know how much Cody now wished they had twenty more things to do before he traveled south. "Admit it. You've enjoyed yourself."

"Maybe a little."

Cody dropped his spoon and it clattered against his nearly empty bowl. It turned a couple of heads, but he didn't pay them any mind because his attention was solely reserved for Jenna. "You know

Grandpa Eddie's watching," he said, pointing up. "I bet he'd say you've enjoyed yourself more than a little."

"I didn't really care for that whole flying in a plane thing," she said with an indifferent shrug. "But the rest . . ."

"Now that you've overcome your fear of public speaking, maybe we should work on conquering your fear of flying," Cody mused. He liked the idea of having a travel companion. Someone special to experience fascinating new places around the globe with. But one glimpse at Graham peering in at them as he stuck his head out the window of Jenna's truck—which they'd taken today because his car was in the shop getting a full service before it went into storage—reminded Cody why she'd likely never leave. It wasn't impossible to travel with a dog, but it was a fairly complicated process in many countries. And he couldn't see Graham—and definitely not Jenna—okay with him hanging out in the cargo hold of a plane.

"Nope, I'm good. One plane ride to and from a glacier lake was enough for one lifetime."

Maybe it was a sign that their attraction and blossoming friendship would never amount to more. That one kiss might be all they ever got. Yes, Cody was planning to spend more time at home in the future. But he couldn't imagine never traveling again. *Or am I just running, like she said?*

"Something wrong with your soup?" Jenna asked, pointing at the spoon he'd abandoned.

"You can't have mine," he said, hugging the bowl toward him in jest, evading her question. "So, three things left. The festival is the easy one. Weather should hold. Not supposed to rain again until Saturday night." *Coincidentally the same time I'm set to get on a plane.* "But the other two . . ."

"I have time today," Jenna said. "We could search around town for Ed."

"Fun fact for you," Cody said after cleaning off his spoon and pointing it at her. "Male moose have a twenty-two-mile home range—in the *summer*. In the winter, that number more than doubles." He filled his spoon again. "We'll be lucky to see Ed before I leave. Might have to talk to Jenkins about loopholes."

"Knowing my grandpa, there aren't any. Or I would've finagled my way out of reading in front of a live studio audience, thank you very much." Jenna pushed her empty bowl to the edge of the table and sat back in the booth. "Okay, that was good."

"See? I told you."

"Maybe you'll just have to stick around Alaska until Ed decides to make an appearance."

"You mean if he stops running off from me every time you show up," he said with a chuckle. "I swear he's doing it to taunt me."

"Because you don't believe in him?" she teased.

"He's not Santa Claus or the Easter Bunny."

"But he's not an ordinary moose, if all the stories about him hold up." Jenna reached for her water, but didn't take a drink. "And there are a *lot* of stories; I've been asking around. Ed's inspired a new character, even if I haven't had the pleasure of actually meeting him."

"I'll tell him next time I see him. Maybe *then* he'll wait until we can get our selfie." Cody emptied the last couple of spoonfuls, wondering what he'd do if Ed continued to be elusive. "I really would stick around longer if I could. But if I don't show up Monday morning, they'll give my job to the next guy in line. My booking agent tells me there's three guys waiting for me not to make it, which means there's actually five." He wouldn't forgive himself for throwing away a job he'd competed really hard to get. Not when it'd change the course of his career, and as a direct result, his life. Or at least that was the wisdom he was so fiercely clinging to.

"Then I suggest we track down this famous moose. Unless you have some hearts to break before you hop on a plane?" Jenna was teasing, but he caught the hint of jealousy lingering in her tone. It normally made him eager to run the other way, but in this instance, it flattered him. Since the night she surprised him with that letter, Jenna was the only one he thought about kissing. He suspected it would be that way for a long time, even an ocean apart.

It could never work between them. They both knew it. Yet here they were with guards down, flirting openly. Acting as if they had all the time in the world to spend together. As if the list would never end. Yes, they often referenced Cody leaving, but it was always in some lighthearted way that avoided the heaviness of the truth. *Maybe it's better this way. Wait until the last minute to face reality.*

"Got some hiking boots? If not, I know a place that sells them." He winked just to hear her magical laugh and commit it to memory.

---

"This is a really impressive store," Jenna said when they were only a few feet inside Evans Outfitters. The high ceilings, partial second floor overlooking the first, and skylights made it feel bigger than it was. "I love the whole log-cabin feel. It's almost . . . cozy in here."

"Family business going on fifty-three years now. My grandpa and his dad started it together. Wanted customers to feel at home." He led them to the shoe section at the back corner of the store, enjoying the way her dark eyes widened and lingered on all the outdoor equipment mounted high on the walls, from fishing poles to snowboards to canoes. She'd never claimed to be an outdoor enthusiast, but her quiet excitement suggested she might just be one at heart.

"Who'll take over after your dad retires?" Jenna asked, stopping to look at a lavender zip-up sweatshirt. She held out the sleeves for inspection.

"Not sure," Cody admitted. About the jacket, he added, "You should try it on."

"Aren't we on a deadline?"

"You remember what Ava said. Ed is only seen when he wants to be seen. A few extra minutes inside isn't going to make a difference to that moose's agenda." Cody caught sight of Dad from the opposite corner, waving him over. With all the time he'd been spending with Jenna these past few days, he hadn't seen much of him. He wasn't worried about it since Dad promised to be the first one on a plane to Maui to visit—aside from Sadie. He was excited about the fishing. "Why don't you try on whatever catches your eye?" he suggested. "I need to talk to my dad for a minute."

"For the record, I still hate shopping."

"Then why are you smiling?"

With quick strides, Cody made it across the store. But before he could ask his dad what was up, Jerry motioned for them to step outside.

The crisp fall breeze greeted them before the door closed. Leaves rustled around them, but Cody couldn't focus on any of the beauty because he felt the unease lingering in the air. "Something wrong, Dad?" His stomach knotted because he recognized the look in his dad's eyes. Something was definitely *not right*.

"I don't want you changing any of your plans, you hear?" Dad's tone was firm and serious as a heart attack. Which Cody was going to have if he didn't just spit it out already. "I mean it."

He wasn't going to make a single promise until he knew what he was dealing with. Or why his dad chose this random moment in time they were never guaranteed. If it weren't for Jenna's whim to search for Ed, Cody wouldn't be standing here right now. "What's going on?"

Dad folded both arms across his chest. "I wasn't going to say anything, but your mother's been pretty insistent."

"Dad, you're scaring me." A million worst-case scenarios rushed through his mind all at once, making Cody a bit dizzy. *Is someone sick? Hurt? Dead?*

"I'm putting the store up for sale."

Cody anticipated a lot of answers—none of them good—but *this* wasn't one of them. "What? Why? Is the store in trouble?" His parents lived a comfortable lifestyle in a nice home. It wasn't anything excessive or extravagant, but it was what they desired. They traveled somewhere new once a year. Drove the vehicles they wanted. They had what they did because of the store's success. He was certain this summer had seen record sales. Cody's own business cleared numbers they'd never seen before. "Or do you need the money for—"

"Calm down." Dad finally cracked a half smile, allowing a fraction of the tension Cody felt to dissipate. "I'm getting old, son. I'm ready to retire, and your mom's nagging me about traveling more. Staying places longer when we do. *That* I blame you for."

"But why sell the store?" The answer came to Cody quicker than Dad could put it into words. "Because none of us want to take it over." At current,

Haylee worked a handful of hours when another family member could watch Melly. Now that Laurel had moved back home, she was taking on more responsibility, too. "I thought you talked to Laurel about an assistant manager position," he said, recalling a conversation he had with his older sister last week.

"Being an assistant manager and owning the store are two very different things. They're going to be parents soon. I want them to focus on that," Dad said, finally unfolding his arms. Reminding Cody of another life event he'd miss out on while in Maui. Laurel and Chase were hoping to adopt a seven-year-old boy by Christmas. His nephew would be ten before he ever met him through something other than Skype or Instagram.

"Look, I'm not putting it up for sale until next spring," Dad continued. "But it's going to happen while you're away and I don't want you to think it might be different if you had stayed. Or cause you to drop everything and come back for the wrong reasons. That's why I'm telling you this now."

"The others don't know?"

"No."

"Not even Laurel?"

"I won't sell it to someone who won't agree to keep her on, if that's what she wants." Dad patted his shoulder. "I don't want to get everyone all worked up for months before anything happens. Keep this between us, okay?"

Cody felt a knot twisting tighter in the pit of his stomach. His dad always dreamed that one of his two sons would want to take over the store. But Marc's calling was as a veterinarian. And Cody's adventurous spirit took him all over the world for months at a time. He'd never envisioned himself tied down to one location, managing a store that sold adventure but didn't allow him to live it. His dad understood and encouraged Cody to follow his desires. "I won't say anything."

"Good. Now, don't you have a *friend* to get back to?"

"Jenna hates shopping," he said, cracking a smile at last.

"You like her."

Cody shrugged. "Hard not to. Almost everyone who meets her likes her."

"Don't play dumb with me. You lose every time." Dad stepped toward the door, but stopped and blocked their path inside. "What happened with Ginny was a long time ago, son. You were both very young. I hope you've let it go by now. Fear only holds you back from some of the best things in life."

"I'm living my best life, Dad. Really." Cody moved around his dad and held the door open. "Besides, you just told me not to change any of my plans."

"Not for my sake or for the store," Dad said as they stepped inside. "I never said anything when it came to *her*." Someone flagged Dad down before Cody closed the door behind them, robbing him of the chance to mine for further insight. He liked Jenna, yes. But enough to throw away the best opportunity he'd ever landed? How many people had he given advice to in similar situations, warning about future resentment? If he stayed, he might be happy in the short-term. But what about five or ten years down the road?

"Okay, so maybe I like shopping more than I thought," Jenna said, her arms overflowing with outdoor clothing.

"I thought we came for hiking boots?"

"We did. They're under all these clothes." She moved around him to the checkout counter and let everything in her arms fall onto it. He caught the shoe box before it tumbled to the floor. "Figured if I'm going to be an Alaskan, I need to look the part."

"You're staying?"

"You sound surprised."

"I didn't realize you were serious already."

"Ninety-eight percent sure at this point." Jenna fished a credit card out of her small over-the-shoulder purse. "Whitney . . . let's just say she crossed a line with me this morning. You're right. I don't have to suffer a toxic relationship with her just because she's blood-related."

Cody's pulse doubled, though he couldn't explain why. Jenna'd been leaning toward staying all week long. Even made a comment about becoming an Alaskan resident a couple times that he didn't take to heart. Until now. Now it sounded so . . . final. "Thought you wanted to see the cabin first?"

"You've seen it," she said as she inserted her card and waited. "If it was a dump inside, you probably would've mentioned that. Especially early on when you were eager to be rid of me."

"I was never eager to be rid of you." He definitely was in the beginning. But now that he'd gotten to know Jenna, he couldn't imagine ever being rid of her. Which was why he was contemplating something crazy himself.

"I can tell when you're lying."

He resisted the urge to help the cashier—some local teenager he didn't recognize—bag up Jenna's purchases. Between Jenna's ability to see through him more thoroughly than an X-ray and his dad's heavy confession, he was craving the fresh air. "I don't want you to get your hopes up about Ed."

"Too late."

"He might—" Cody's phone rang, and for once, he didn't mind the interruption. "Hey, it's Sadie. I better take this. Meet you outside?"

"Of course."

He'd never met a woman who went with the flow as easily as Jenna, unless they were trying to impress him in hopes for something more serious than a date or two. As much as he still couldn't read her all that well, he knew she wasn't doing a single thing to impress him. Aside, possibly, from some extra mascara that brought out her eyes. He didn't mind that one bit.

"Cody?" Sadie sobbed into the phone.

"What's wrong?"

"I need you to come get me."

There wasn't one second Cody hesitated in his decision to drive to Anchorage. He only wondered how he'd break the news to Jenna. "Where are you?"

"I'm in this crappy hotel." She sniffled. "You can't tell anyone."

His protective brotherly instincts took hold, and his pulse raced for an entirely different reason this time. If her on-again-off-again whatever he was now —*better be an ex*—laid a finger on Sadie, a side of him that rarely reared its ugly head would come out. "Okay."

"I mean it, Cody."

"I know."

Jenna emerged from the store, but her smile dropped when she spotted his grim expression. He *felt* her concern more than sensed it. She'd forgive him for canceling their plans last-minute. It reminded him of something Eddie once shared with Cody about the love of his life.

"Text me the address."

Jenna touched his arm gently, her compassion reaching him on a soul level. He didn't believe in things like this. In soulmates and falling in love with someone you just met. He'd starred in enough movies that played up these fantasies, reminding him all too often how far they were from reality. Yet he couldn't deny this connection that only deepened with each passing day.

"I'll be there as soon as I can."

"Please hurry."

"You know I will."

"Okay. Cody?"

"Yeah?"

"Thank you." So much was packed into those two words. If this had happened a week later, he wouldn't be so readily available to save the day. He had no idea what he would find when he arrived in Anchorage, but his sister needed him. That was what mattered. They'd deal with everything else once he got there.

"Don't leave your room or let anyone else in."

Jenna stood patiently by, still holding bags in one hand. "You need to go."

"I'm sorry to cancel our Ed search—"

"You're wasting time." She opened the back door of her truck and clipped Graham's leash onto his collar. Jenna handed Cody her truck keys once the pup leapt out of the back seat.

"I can't take your truck. What are you going to drive?"

"The lodge is only a few blocks away. We'll walk."

"I can't—"

"You can't drive *your* car when it's on a hoist."

He'd forgotten his car was in the shop for a full service, but Jenna hadn't. And she hadn't hesitated to do something selfless about it. *It would be so easy to fall the rest of the way . . .* "I'm sorry about Ed—"

"This is more important, right?"

"Yeah, it is."

She reached for his hand, squeezing it. "Then go. I'll be here when you get back."

# CHAPTER TWELVE

Jenna

Jenna's arms were tired after the uphill walk back to the lodge carrying all her purchases while Graham zigzagged on the leash, but she had no regrets loaning her truck to Cody in his time of need. She considered it fate that she had a full tank of gas when she handed over the keys.

Leaving her shopping bags untouched on a sitting chair, she sat on the bed and rolled her aching shoulders. "Guess that's what I get for *shopping* like a normal person," she said to a sleepy Graham. The pup was sprawled out in the middle of the bed, leaving her barely enough room for her legs if she crossed them at the ankles.

Cody ought to be halfway to Anchorage by now. He hadn't called, not that he likely had cell service in the mountains. He didn't *owe* her a phone call. They weren't a couple, much as the idea had danced around in her fantasies lately. They were friends with some . . . complicated feelings. But it didn't mean he needed to call Jenna with a status report. Or to talk through whatever he was feeling with her.

It left her anxious and stir-crazy.

If this was what being in love felt like in tough moments such as these, she wasn't so sure she wanted it. Remembering that toe-curling kiss, though, made her understand why some people leapt blindly and head-first into any chance at love. The mere memory or the way she craved a repeat performance was enough to make her forget anything uncomfortable or hard.

"I'm not in love," Jenna said to herself. Then she said it again to Graham. The dog looked either unconvinced or unimpressed. *Probably both.*

"Okay, I need to get back to this moose story."

Graham groaned and stretched all four legs at once.

Determined to keep her mind off subjects that would only make her restless, she spread her sketches out around the dog to decide which elements she liked best in each of the different cartoonish moose she'd drawn. She'd promised her agent and editor both a final sketch of her newest leading character by the end of the week, but she still wasn't quite happy with any one version she'd drafted. Nor had she settled on a name. "Maybe it would help if I actually met this Ed character since he's the inspiration."

The chime on her phone nearly sent her flying off the bed. Graham jumped up with a grumpy old man growl at the disturbance, stepping on a sketch. Jenna's phone landed on the floor with a *thud*.

She quickly gathered the scattered papers before Graham could puncture any of them with his claws, and her phone chimed again.

Her heart pounded as she recovered it from the floor.

But it wasn't Cody's name on the screen.

**Whitney:** Are you ready to apologize yet?

**Whitney:** It's time to grow up, Jenna. Just say you're sorry so we can finalize my wedding plans. This has gone on long enough. No need to keep being a child about it.

Jenna felt something akin to fury flood her veins. "She's unbelievable." The only reason she left the line of communication open was because of her pitiful hope that Whitney would come to her senses and apologize to her. That for once, her older sister would believe her when she told her the truth. Especially in a situation that involved something as serious as marriage.

It wasn't fair to try so hard to make something work and *still* feel like a failure at the end of it. How many times had she wished she had the type of sister she could share everything with? What she wouldn't give for her and Whitney to be close. To know she could tell her all about Cody and actually get half-decent advice in return. A tear rolled down her cheek as she mourned the loss of a dream that would never be realized.

Jenna steeled her heart, refusing to shed another tear for the relationship she was about to end. "I've done everything I can, right, Graham Cracker?"

Having recovered from the initial shock of being pulled from his half-slumber state, he thumped his tail twice against the comforter. *Guess that's a yes.*

**Jenna:** I love you, Whitney. But I can't do this anymore. I'm blocking your number.

If a true emergency arose, several people who claimed to be her friend still had this number and could reach Jenna. But she still felt a twist of guilt when she selected the option to block Whitney, carrying out her promise to prove it wasn't an empty threat.

Graham, sensing she was distraught, crawled into her lap. She hugged him as the tears fell, and suddenly she was crying for more than just the loss of a sister. She missed Grandpa. She wished he were here to tell her what to do. She missed Cody, even though he hadn't really left yet. But he would be. She wanted to ask him to stay, but she'd never forgive herself if he did as she asked and resented her down the road for it.

Jenna hated feeling this vulnerable, but she couldn't stop the overwhelming rush of emotion.

She cried for what felt like hours, but in reality, was only half of one. When the tears dried up, Graham's poor fur was soaked. The loyal pup didn't seem to mind. "How did I get so lucky to find you?"

He licked her hand, then her cheek. She giggled and he licked it again.

"Okay, okay. We'll go for a *fun* walk." She slipped on her tennis shoes, grabbed a jacket and his leash, and headed out the back door.

They'd been making regular trips to Lookout Point, even when the sun wasn't setting. It was windier up here than in town, which was why she suspected they had the trail to themselves. She liked it that way. The silence granted her permission to be still. To let go of everything that burdened her.

Graham let out a whine when a gust of wind shook a loose fence rail. "It's okay, buddy. It's just the wind." But when he whined again, she realized he was looking behind them.

Jenna's heart thumped, terrified she was going to turn around and see a bear. Cadence had warned her to be on the lookout for them. Black bears were rarely sighted, but they *had* been seen on occasion.

But it wasn't a bear behind them.

It was a massive moose with enormous antlers. If he charged them, she was going off a cliff for sure. Her heart thundered in her chest as Graham whined again. At least her dog was sticking close to her side instead of doing his *let me at 'em* pacing. That might be the only reason the creature hadn't moved.

"Wait. Are you—" The moose tilted his head and her eyes went wide. "You're Ed." Countless people had mentioned the beast's doglike head tilt in the Ed-encounter stories she'd collected. It was one of his trademark gestures that distinguished him from other moose. "It's really you."

They stared at one another for several moments as the moose leisurely stripped the bark from a branch. Jenna wasn't sure what she expected to happen. Cody was right; Ed wasn't Santa Claus. She'd probably scream and tumble down the cliff behind her in shock if Ed starting talking.

"Everyone says you show up at the most inconvenient times, but I don't know what that means for me. Well, except Cody's not with me and this won't count for the list." She was talking to a moose. If anyone from Indiana saw her now, they'd probably have her committed. The thought made her smirk, reminding her she still had a two-week notice to submit. Something she was doing the second she got back to the lodge room. "Everyone who's met you has some profound love story to share. All because you intervened somehow. What message are you trying to send me?"

Ed blinked as he stared down the trail, almost as

if in thought. Except, moments later, he reached for another branch to nibble.

*He's a moose, Jenna. There's no message.*

---

Cody

Cody never performed stunts with cars, but he drove to Anchorage as though he'd mastered in Formula One speed and precision. Without cell reception most of the drive, he couldn't check on Sadie, so speed was his best and only ally. He had no idea what he was walking into. His sister had cried wolf enough times in her life to make everyone else in the family hardly bat an eye when something went wrong.

But Cody worried that if he accepted that as well, the one time she truly needed someone, no one would be there. The one time it might mean life or death, she'd be on her own. He'd never forgive himself if it came to that.

*I'll never let that happen.*

No one knew about the times he'd left a movie set halfway around the world to fly back for Sadie's sake. Though both times had been for minor issues, they'd been major crises to her. She'd needed him to help put her broken pieces back together. He had no regrets because he understood his sister better than anyone. Better, he suspected, than she knew herself.

Which was why this time, after he confirmed she was in no immediate danger, he was switching tactics and forcing tough love on her instead.

As the outskirts of the city came into view, a series of pings sounded on his phone. He waited until snagged behind a string of cars to check the texts. All were from Sadie, and to his relief, all were texts he expected. *Are you almost here? I'm hungry. I'm sorry I put you through this. You're the only one who cares. Can we get ice cream?*

Cody typed out a quick text with one hand to let Sadie know he was close. Then, without forethought, he dialed Jenna's number.

She picked up on the first ring. "Is she okay?"

Cody let out a heavy sigh of relief at the sound of Jenna's voice. The way she put his sister first instead of herself stirred emotions inside him he swore he'd never let himself feel again. "I'm almost there. I think she is, but I won't know for sure until I have eyes on her."

He yearned for the consoling caress of her fingers as they threaded through his. That comforting squeeze that reassured him they were in this together. Her words confirmed it. "I'm here to help however I can. Just tell me if there's anything I can do."

"You've already helped. You didn't even hesitate to lend me your truck." He lifted the corner of his mouth, but his rearview mirror revealed that his usually carefree smile was forlorn. How would he help Sadie all the way from Maui when he wouldn't have more than forty-eight hours off at any given time? The contract was very specific about expectations, and there was less wiggle room with it than Eddie's bucket list. "You didn't ask questions. How did—"

"I just . . . knew."

"She's not on drugs," Cody said, pulling into the parking lot of the hotel in the middle of Anchorage. At least it wasn't some rundown motel on the outskirts. He'd made Sadie promise never to hide out at one again after the last time he found her in one. "I know when my sister's lying to me, and I know when she's telling me the truth. She's never lied to me about that. I don't know why it's so important you know that, but it is. Whatever's happened to her—"

"I believe you, Cody."

"Thank you."

"Will you let me know when you're on your way back?" Her kind, considerate tone nearly did him in. Jenna could be cold as ice, but she had the biggest heart of anyone he'd ever met. It wasn't a matter of *if* he was falling in love. In this one conversation, he realized he already had. He had no idea what he was going to do about it.

"Of course."

"Go get your sister."

He shoved open the door and rushed into the lobby, heading straight for the elevator to the sixth floor. But the elevator was taking too long to travel back to the ground level, so he opted for the stairs and took them three at a time.

Cody was panting by the time he reached Sadie's hotel room, but he was here. That's what mattered. He knocked on the door. "Sadie? It's me. It's—" The door opened slowly and a redheaded woman with streaks of mascara running down her cheeks threw herself into Cody's arms. Sadie was only recognizable through her distraught appearance because he'd found her this way before. *Too many times.*

"You're here."

"Of course, I'm here. Where's your stuff?"

"I only have one bag." She pointed toward the edge of the disheveled bed and went to grab it. It was then that Cody took in Sadie's appearance. The tight red dress she tried to hide beneath a fuzzy black sweater. Her feet were bare, but red lines from where her high heels pressed in were visible. Though her hair was tossed into a lopsided messy bun, he noticed the prominent curls Sadie had likely spent hours perfecting the night before.

Sadie hooked her stilettos with a couple of fingers and headed to the door, but Cody stopped her with a hand on both shoulders. He searched his sister for bruises or cuts. "Are you hurt?"

"Only my pride, Cody."

His protective brotherly instincts took over, and he refused to move out of her way until she looked him in the eye. "Are you sure?"

She rolled up one sleeve, then the other. Aside

from a new flower tattoo, she was unscathed. "Happy?"

Happy was the last word he'd used to describe how he felt. Relief might be more accurate. "Let's go."

"Where are we going?"

During his long, quiet drive, Cody had loads of time to contemplate how to answer the question he knew Sadie would ask almost right away. Most times, he took her back to her apartment so she could shower. Then they'd grab a bite to eat or catch a movie. Sometimes, they stayed in and feasted on microwave popcorn while Sadie tried to pick him out in movies.

But one thing was becoming very clear to him. He wasn't helping Sadie; he was enabling her to repeat her past immature behavior. He could do one more favor for her before he left, even if she ended up hating him for it.

"Cody?" she asked again in the elevator.

"Are you going to tell me what happened?" He couldn't bring her back to Sunset Ridge in that scandalous dress. Mom might have a heart attack, and Dad might go on a murderous rage. But if he made a detour to her apartment, his plan might unravel. No, they had to head straight back. With any luck, he could sneak her inside the house—where she had clothes in her old room to change into—and burn that dress before anyone else ever saw it.

"Over ice cream?"

He didn't answer as they headed for the truck.

"Whose is this? Did Marc get a new truck—hey, you promised not to tell anyone!" Tears streaked down her cheeks. He was certain they weren't the last ones he'd see today. Oh, no. When his sister figured out what he was really up to, she'd cry a river.

"A friend let me borrow it."

Sadie got in and tossed her bag in the back. "A girlfriend?" She tried to tease him through the sniffles. At least her sense of humor wasn't completely broken. She'd need it for all the hard work ahead.

"She's a *friend*."

"You didn't say *just* a friend," Sadie countered after she blew her nose. "She means something to you."

Cody didn't respond to that, because he didn't know how. Yes, Jenna meant a whole lot to him. But admitting it didn't solve anything. He'd spent as much time on that drive thinking about his Jenna-slash-Maui predicament as he had about Sadie. No conclusion had magically jumped out at him.

He was almost desperate enough to find Ed and demand an answer. *From a moose.* Cody scrubbed a hand over his face, convinced he was losing his mind.

"Wait, where are you going?" Sadie asked when he turned in the opposite direction of her apartment. "Cody!"

"Home."

"I can't go back there," Sadie said between sniffles, panic dancing in her eyes as she practically crawled up the seat and reached for the road behind them. She was definitely the most dramatic Evans sibling, that was for certain. "No one will understand."

"I might. If you start talking."

"Will you turn around if I do?"

Cody stared straight ahead, because crocodile tears or not, he couldn't stand to see them streaming down any woman's cheeks—especially one of his sisters. He'd have to be coldhearted to do what was best for her right now. "No."

"Take me to Maui with you," Sadie begged between sobs. "*Please*, Cody."

"I can't do that."

"I can't go back to Sunset Ridge."

"You can't keep running from your problems. I've allowed you to do it for too long." Cody's tone was both calm and firm. Anger fizzled on the surface, but Sadie didn't seem to notice how upset he truly was. Mostly, he was angry at himself for waiting so long to take drastic measure. All this time, he kept hoping Sadie would grow up on her own. "The longer you keep running from everything instead of facing it, the worse it'll be."

"You mean the same way you keep running away?" The snap in her tone might catch most people off guard, but Cody hardly blinked. Her temper and smart mouth were Sadie's next line of defense. The same things that kept her in the hottest water with the rest of the family because, unlike Cody, they took everything she said personally.

"You have two choices," Cody said, glancing back at Sadie through the rearview mirror. "I can sneak you into Mom and Dad's tonight to get a good night's sleep before you face them in the morning. Or, I can wake up the whole house when we get there and risk giving Mom a heart attack at the way you're dressed."

"It was for an office party," Sadie snapped. Maybe this wasn't the on-again-off-again boyfriend. Maybe this was something else. "Not that it matters anyway. I got fired. *There*. Are you happy? You're dragging me back to the place I hate the most at my absolute lowest."

"I love you, Sadie," Cody said as he passed the last stoplight out of Anchorage and headed south. "But if you want me to keep being there for you, it's time for you to grow up and do the right thing. The *hard* thing."

# CHAPTER THIRTEEN

Jenna

It was well after midnight when Jenna's phone rang. Groggily, she reached toward the nightstand. It took her three attempts to successfully hit the answer button. "Hello?"

"Hey." Cody's gentle tone caused her heart to flutter. Suddenly, she wasn't so tired. A sleepy Graham perked one ear from his spot on the edge of his bed, and her heart melted. Her *dog* loved Cody. How was that not a sign? "Sorry it's so late."

"Did you make it back?"

"Yeah, we're home." The way he said those words warmed her soul, though she knew better than to read into anything after the long day he had. Cody was likely tired and a sliver delirious. Sunset Ridge would likely always feel like home to him, even if it was only a home base.

"Is Sadie—"

"Snuck her inside to get some sleep before the family gets hold of her tomorrow morning. If you want to see the real show, join us for breakfast." His chuckle was only half-hearted. Sadie'd need an ally and they both knew it. "Can you come outside?"

"Now?"

"Yeah."

"I thought you were at home."

"I'm out back. Behind the lodge."

"Like some creepy stalker?" Jenna teased, slipping on a pair of fuzzy slippers and a hoodie. She glanced at Graham, but all he did was stretch with his eyes closed and roll onto his opposite side. The pup didn't seem worried about her late-night rendezvous and, if she was being honest, she didn't mind having Cody all to herself. "Should I be worried?"

"I promise it'll be worth it. Just hurry up before it's too late."

Exhausted or not, Jenna didn't dare waste what little time she had left with him. Never mind that every memory they created together would only make it that much harder to let him go. Or that every minute spent with him gave her hope that he might change his mind about leaving at all. "This better be nicer than the last surprise."

"Oh, it is."

She ended the call and left her cell on the nightstand. Quietly, she crept down the hall, traveling the same route she used to take Graham outside. Cody was waiting for her a few feet from the door, looking completely relaxed and not a bit worn out in his jeans and Carhartt jacket hanging open. "Hurry up, slowpoke."

She rolled her eyes at him, but the gesture was pointless in the darkness. "What's so special out here?" she asked, folding her arms over her chest when the frosty breeze cut through her sweatshirt.

"Number four."

"Four what?"

Cody pointed straight up, the simple gesture drawing her gaze to the night sky. Vibrant greens and purples danced overhead. She stared, mesmerized at how alive the moving colors seemed to be. "It's like someone's using a paintbrush." A fluid streak would appear, then disappear, almost as if erased and replaced by new colorful streaks. Everything moved so much faster than she expected. Tears of awe gathered in the corners of her eyes. She'd never seen anything more beautiful. "They're so much brighter than I expected—so *close*."

"You're in Alaska now. Better get used to it."

"Oh, I definitely can."

"C'mon." Cody held out his hand for her. "The view's even better from Lookout Point."

She slid her icy fingers into his warm hand, threading her fingers through his until they locked together. She never wanted to let go. For tonight, she'd forget that she'd have to. It was easier that way.

She marveled at the rapidly moving lights as she followed his lead down the trail. "Did I tell you I saw Ed today?"

"You're kidding."

"Graham and I came out here earlier. Ed surprised us."

Cody let out a low laugh that made those butterflies wake right up from their slumber. "Go figure."

"I asked him if he had a message for me, but he didn't have much to say. He just sort of stared at me and blinked."

"Yeah, he does that."

"And the head tilt!" Jenna added excitedly. "He may not be some insightful talking moose, but he totally did the head tilt everyone talks about."

"I wonder if Jenkins would accept that we've both seen him, just not *together*," Cody mused as they approached the familiar fence. Though the trail started in the lodge's backyard, Jenna had been reassured it was open to the public. She planned to make many more visits to her new favorite place.

"I was so shocked that I forgot to pull out my phone. Well, honestly, I was backed up against the fence worried that Graham would spook him and we'd all tumble down a cliff when Ed charged. That guy is *huge*! Way bigger than I expected."

When Cody stopped in the clearing, he tugged on her hand to spin her around. She collided against his chest, catching herself with her palm. It wasn't intentional that her hand slipped through the opening in his jacket and landed flat against his shirt. But she wasn't complaining about the hard, sculpted muscle she felt through the chilled cotton fabric.

"May I have this dance, Jenna Kingsley?"

"We don't have any music." She stepped closer to him. "Wait, don't tell me you're going to sing. It would make sense that you have an amazing voice that drives your fan club even crazier about you."

Cody laughed as he placed her arms around his neck, then dropped his own to her waist. "My singing voice is terrible enough to send the northern lights away. I'm not risking it." He reached into his jacket pocket for his phone. She expected him to snap a picture, but instead, he turned on a slow song. One she'd heard on the radio during her long drive to Alaska, but not often enough to know its name. She didn't care. The happy ballad gave her the perfect excuse to tuck herself against him.

Jenna nestled her cheek against his chest, catching a whiff of his woodsy with a hint of aquatic cologne. She inhaled deeply, committing the scent to memory.

Here in Cody's arms, the world felt right in a way it rarely had. Everything in her life was changing. Everyone who'd been a part of it was gone in one fashion or another—except Graham Cracker. All of it should terrify her, but instead, she felt excited for the unknown. Invincible and fearless to start a new chapter of her life on her own terms. She'd call the shots and never again allow herself to feel unfairly guilty.

*If only Cody would stay.*

"Hey," Cody whispered, tracing a finger across her jaw. She didn't understand how his hands were warm, but she appreciated the way they transferred heat throughout her body so she could stand the chilly night air longer. "We need a picture."

"Do we?" She'd rather nestle closer against him and keep dancing to the random playlist of ballads.

"The lights won't stay out forever. They tend to disappear. Some nights they come back for another round or two. Some nights—"

"—they don't." She stopped rocking long enough for him to snap a few pictures. Who knew whether they'd turn out. Hopefully they'd satisfy Jenkins. Maybe they'd have to try again.

Cody dropped the phone back in his jacket pocket, the music no longer playing. But he held on to her just the same. "That's officially number four."

"Only two more—" A long yawn Jenna couldn't fight escaped.

"Two left." Jenna might be imagining the forlorn tone. It was late, and she was sleepy. She wanted to believe he was falling in love with her, too, but the timing couldn't be any worse.

"I bet you're eager to get the keys to your grand-pa's cabin."

"I am ready to unpack the trailer," she admitted,

still swaying with him as she watched the magical display overhead. He was right. It was fading. Soon, she suspected the lights would be gone. Maybe for an hour. Maybe for the night.

"I think they're about done," Cody said, noticing the dimming lights as well. "You better get some sleep." He pressed a gentle kiss to her forehead that made her skin tingle with delight. "Festival starts at nine. We have a *lot* to see."

"Do we really have to spend *all* day there?"

"There's not another festival until spring. So, yes." He cupped her cheek and drew her in for a gentle, sensual kiss that made her toes curl and her heart soar. She shouldn't let it fill her with hope, but it did just the same.

"Cody?"

"C'mon. Let's get you back. I'm fading fast." He draped an arm over her shoulder and steered her down the path toward the lodge. "I'm going to need all my energy for the morning when my family discovers I brought Sadie home unannounced."

It was late and they were both tired, so she forced herself to practice patience and didn't press. Grandpa always told her *love will find a way when it's true.* Maybe, just maybe, there was a way to work this out.

# CHAPTER FOURTEEN

CODY

"If Mr. Jenkins isn't satisfied by the three thousand pictures we took at the Harvest Festival, I give up," Jenna said with an easy laugh from the passenger seat of her truck. Cody was getting used to driving it, making him consider getting his own.

"The only thing we could've done to make it more convincing was to invite him to tag along." Cody glanced in the rearview mirror at a happy-go-lucky Graham darting from one half-open window to another. The pup who was accustomed to riding shotgun now happily hopped in the back seat when he rode with both Jenna and Cody. He'd always loved dogs, but with his lifestyle, owning one wasn't a possibility. Now, he couldn't imagine hanging out in Maui without getting sneak-licked by the pup. "We hit *every* booth. Sampled every food vendor. Played all the games—twice."

"Thank you for the stuffed moose, by the way— even if he *is* green."

"Better than hot pink."

Staying had never weighed heavier on his mind than it had today.

First, there was the family breakfast that could've aired as a pilot episode of a new reality show. *Everyone* had an opinion about Sadie's unexpected appearance at the table. For once, she resisted the typical urge to snap back at everyone. Well, everyone except Haylee. Those two might never see eye to eye.

But would Sadie's path to maturity stay on course if he left? She struggled to commit to hard things, and he wouldn't be around to guide her back on course should she stray.

Then there was Melly. Oh, his heart, that baby girl knew how to get him hook, line, and sinker. She had only to lock those sparkling eyes on him and giggle to melt his heart. He couldn't stop thinking about missing her first steps. Could he teach her to say *Cody* via FaceTime?

Laurel and Chase had finally gotten to meet the little boy they hoped to adopt by Christmas. His sister was so excited to tell him all about his nephew who loved all things outdoors. But Cody didn't want to wait three years to make good on his promise to take the kid fishing.

Then there was still the matter of Dad selling the store in the spring that bothered him. Never mind that Cody wasn't interested in owning a store that'd anchor him in Sunset Ridge for certain. But maybe if he stuck around, he could help buy more time to figure out a family-oriented solution.

"A lot on your mind?" Jenna asked, her tone light-hearted enough to *almost* fool him. But he was figuring her out better with each day they spent together. She was searching for answers about their future. Answers he would give her soon.

"Still have to pack up a few things," he said, careful not to meet her assessing gaze. He wasn't lying, but he wasn't being completely forthcoming either. "Get a few things ready so my parents can mail them to me once I'm settled." Though most of his things sat in his room ready to go, he'd put packing that final box to the last minute, blaming the bucket list. But deep down, he suspected he'd sensed the truth days ago. He didn't want to leave. Not this time.

"How much time do we still have to kill?" Jenna asked when he hung out at a stop sign several moments longer than necessary.

"Fifteen minutes. Unless Haylee gives me the signal sooner." He couldn't have convinced Mom to abandon her surprise going-away party plans if he tried. The closer the event got, the more a radical idea tempted him. With everyone gathered in one place, he could announce he was staying.

His career would be over—Haylee would post about it on Instagram before he had a chance to call Holden with the news. His days traveling the globe for months at a time would be through. He'd have to stop running.

But he'd be home.

Home with his family.

Home with the woman he loved.

"Is that Haylee?" Jenna asked, pointing to his phone. He'd been so lost in thought he hadn't heard the ping.

"Yep, that's our cue." He reached for her hand, squeezing it. All day, he'd been tempted to tell her the news. Tell her they had all the time in the world to finally spot Ed together and finish out the list. But he had to be one hundred percent sure before he breathed a word. It might be fun if Jenna was as surprised as everyone else.

He rolled forward through the intersection, headed for his parents' home.

"Remember," Jenna said, "act surprised."

"You too."

She chuckled. "You know I'm in on this too, right?"

Cody rarely felt nervous about making an announcement, but tonight, his pulse wouldn't stop racing. He'd socialized at the backyard party for well over two hours. It was when the last piece of cake disappeared that his palms began to sweat. Soon, people would start leaving. If he was going to tell everyone his decision, he needed to do it soon.

But first, he needed some air.

Several short trails snaked through the wooded area behind his parents' property, and he took one of them that led to a small clearing with a spectacular view of the star-filled sky.

It wasn't the announcement about staying that had him so worked up. He'd decided Sunset Ridge was where he wanted to be. Maybe it wasn't some sandy beach. Yes, he'd have to endure winter in the arctic without a clue how to spend it. But time with the people who mattered most—no adrenaline rush or seven-figure paycheck could give that back to him.

It was the second part of that announcement that had him feeling like a nervous teenager.

The part that involved Jenna.

Because if he was going to change his entire life, he wasn't going to do it halfway. He was going to lay it all on the line and confess he'd fallen in love with her, even if such a strong admission to a woman he'd hardly known a week sent her running. Jenna had the power to crush his heart, whether she realized it or not. Deep down, he didn't believe she would.

He was no longer some young lovestruck teenager who was incapable of realizing the girl he was crazy about wasn't crazy about him.

Jenna wasn't Ginny.

"Hiding from your fan club?" Jenna's teasing voice startled him, but only for a moment before it soothed him. Yes, he could definitely handle hearing that sweet voice for a long time to come.

"Stalking me?"

"What if I am?"

He reached for her hand automatically, reveling in the way her soft skin felt against his rough palms. His gaze dropped to her lips, tempting him to steal a kiss while they still had some privacy. Once he made his announcement, he'd be bombarded with excitement and questions. He took a step closer and lowered his head.

"Cody, look!" Jenna pointed behind him, her eyes wide and excited. "I don't believe it. It's Ed!"

Slowly, as to not startle the elusive beast, Cody turned to follow her finger. Only through the faint glow from the outdoor party lights could he make out the moose and his goofy head tilt. "What do you know."

"Number five."

"Number five indeed." As he reached for his phone, sloth-like and cautious, Cody felt a pang of mourning. He wished as he had dozens of times earlier in the week, that the list was longer. It shouldn't matter, considering his change in plans. But the excitement he expected to feel when they finally completed the list didn't come.

"Cody, there's another moose."

"What?"

"Back in the trees." She slowly raised her arm and pointed. "It doesn't have antlers, though."

"Ed, you sly devil," Cody said, unable to quiet his laugh. "No wonder you keep running off. You have a girlfriend."

"Moose date? C'mon. *That* is a stretch for me."

"It's rutting season. Turn around. We need that picture before he runs off after his new love." Cody lifted his phone, positioning them in the photo to capture Ed before his animal instincts sent him running after the cow. He snapped three pictures before Ed pivoted and trotted toward the female moose.

"What is rutting season?" Jenna asked when he lowered the phone.

"Moose mating season."

"Oh. *Oh*."

"It's the only time of year you'll see a bull moose hanging around other moose. They're usually pretty lone creatures."

"Oh, my goodness, is there going to be a Little Ed —or Edwina—in the spring?" Jenna squealed in delight.

"Edwina?"

"Do we get to name it?"

"There you two are," Haylee said, her tone exasperated. "I've been looking everywhere. You're going to miss the movie I made."

"Movie?"

Haylee let out an annoyed sigh as she tugged on Cody's wrist. "I worked on it all week. You're not hiding in the woods for the premiere." When Jenna didn't immediately follow, Haylee looked back at her. "You too, Jenna. I need your help with something."

# CHAPTER FIFTEEN

Jenna

Jenna traveled down the long basement hall in search of Haylee's room, amazed at how enormous the log home truly was. She could practically hear the laughter, bickering, and excited voices talking on top of one another from years past. It was a home filled with love and acceptance. The same type of home she'd always wished she'd grown up in herself.

The same type of home she wanted to someday raise a family of her own in.

A slightly frazzled Haylee'd sent her inside in search of the presentation clicker she'd forgotten in her bedroom. Jenna counted three doors on the left, but at the second stopped in her tracks. The door stood halfway open, giving her a peek at stuffed duffle bags lined against one wall.

She should leave well enough alone. Haylee would figure out the projection issue any moment and need that presentation clicker to start showing a movie Jenna definitely didn't want to miss. But she was lured inside anyway.

When the door swung open, Jenna silently gasped.

Four stuffed duffle bags stood against one wall. A dozen boxes against another. One was open and few things scattered around the floor beside it. The room was nearly bare aside from the bed being made, a sweatshirt draped on the footboard, and a coffee cup on the nightstand. It was possible he'd been packed since the day they met. Possible that he still planned to stay but hadn't *unpacked*. But it was also possible Cody was getting on that plane tomorrow and there was nothing she could—or *should*—do to stop it.

A cheer from outside reminded her of the urgent mission Haylee'd given her. Jenna started to back out of the room, but she caught something sticking out of the nightstand drawer. She should leave well enough alone. She wasn't one to snoop. Yet she pulled the drawer open without recollection of walking all the way into the room.

A corner of a printed document had been sticking out of the drawer—a contract.

Jenna knew she shouldn't touch it, but she'd already pulled it from the drawer. It wasn't just Cody's name that jumped out at her, it was the *three million dollar* amount they promised to pay him. She gasped. Though Jenna had no idea what a good stuntman was paid, she couldn't fathom one earning that kind of money. If he didn't get on that plane, he'd forfeit a fortune. That was life-changing money. When Cody said this job could open doors for him, she hadn't realized that *this* was what he meant. He could do anything he wanted after the show.

But he had to go.

"He likes you, you know." The woman's voice caused Jenna to let out a quick scream. She turned to find a redhead with sea-green eyes—just like Cody's—studying her curiously. "But he wouldn't be happy here long-term."

"You must be Sadie."

Sadie folded her arms and leaned her weight against the door frame as Jenna put the contract back into the drawer and closed it. Her hands were shaky and her pulse was out of control, but it had nothing to do with being caught snooping. Judging from Sadie's expression, she'd already seen it.

"Cody tried staying here one winter when he was twenty-two. After he'd broken three ribs. Did he tell you that?"

Jenna recalled the dramatic way Sadie's siblings had described her, and the grace Cody always gave in her defense, claiming she was misunderstood. None of it helped her now in Jenna's own assessment. Sadie seemed like a wildcard, her very presence warning Jenna to keep her guard up. "No."

"He was miserable. There's nothing for him here

in the winter. His kayak shop is closed, and he hates working at the store. He couldn't work on any sets that season, but he booked a ticket out of here after three weeks of going stir-crazy. We didn't see him again until it was time to open his shop."

"Why are you telling me this?"

"Because I don't think you should ask him to stay."

"How do you—"

"I've been watching you two all night. Anyone with eyes can see there's something between you. I know you care about him, so I'm asking you *not* to hold him back from what truly makes him happy." Sadie held up the clicker Jenna had been sent inside to find. "Because if you ask him to stay, he will."

Jenna took the presentation clicker from Sadie with shaky hands and darted down the hall. She didn't need the rest spelled out. She and Cody would be happy for a short time before resentment took over. He'd always wonder if he should've gone to Maui and what he gave up because he didn't. She wasn't going to stand in someone else's way of their dreams and live with that guilt. Not ever again.

"I thought you got lost!" Haylee said, yanking the clicker from Jenna's hand in the kitchen upstairs. "The movie was about to start, but the alarm went off at the store and Dad had to go check it out. Now we have to wait until he gets back."

"Sorry I took—"

"It's fine, seriously." Haylee's reassuring smile gave Jenna hope that she might still have allies in the Evans clan after what she was about to do. *Maybe.*

"I'll meet you outside," Jenna said, waving Haylee on.

She waited until she heard the creaking on the stairs warning her Sadie was following her before she forced herself outside.

Jenna wove her way through the crowd, but didn't know where she was going. She felt sick to her stomach. All day long, she'd gotten the distinct impression that Cody wanted to stay in Sunset Ridge, even though he never came out and said it. It was in the half-hearted ways he talked about packing and being on the set. In the way his eyes lit up talking about his new nephew he couldn't wait to take fishing. In the way he kept sending his booking agent to voicemail.

But what if Sadie was right?

What if he only *thought* he'd be happy here when in reality he'd be miserable two months down the road? Could she live with that guilt, knowing she was the reason he forfeited not just a chance at a boatload of money, but his entire career? She knew enough about the entertainment industry from her grandpa's stories to know that one unpopular decision could blacklist you from future work. If he gave up this gig to stay with her, he'd give up everything he loved without the possibility of getting it back.

"Ms. Kingsley, lovely to see you here tonight."

Jenna looked up to find Mr. Jenkins standing directly in front of her. Another couple of steps and she'd have plowed right into him and spilled his drink all over his suit.

"Mr. Jenkins, hey."

"How are you and Cody coming on that list? I've been combing the document for loopholes, but—"

"We just finished it tonight." *This feels like a sign.*

"You did?"

"I have some of the pictures, but Cody has the rest on his phone." As if speaking his name had summoned him, Cody appeared beside her. Her heart thundered in her chest, as if angered at what she was about to do. *You're doing this because you love him. Love is about sacrifice. That's what Grandpa always said.*

"Mr. Jenkins, just the man I was hoping to run into tonight. Jenna's ready for those cabin keys as soon as you can squeeze us in."

"Considering you're leaving tomorrow, why don't we meet down there tonight? Shouldn't take long if you two have all the photos?"

"There's no need to rush—"

"Tonight would be great. The sooner the better." It took everything she had to shove down her true feelings and mask them with the same icy demeanor she'd used as armor when she first arrived in Sunset Ridge. But it was a necessary evil if she wanted Cody to believe she didn't care about him.

"I thought the beds at the lodge were crazy comfortable," Cody teased.

*They were.* "This has always been about me getting my grandpa's cabin, Cody. Nothing more." It was only because she'd spent years steeling her emotions with Whitney that she could pull it off now as hurt and confusion swam in those sea-green eyes. "I appreciate your help. I'm not going to waste another minute of your time. Let's get this over with so you can go to Maui, and I can get into my grandpa's cabin."

"Jenna, can we talk?" Cody asked, reaching for her elbow.

She pulled it away because his touch would make her lose her nerve. "There's nothing to talk about."

"Actually, there *is*."

Jenna sensed curious eavesdroppers. As much as she yearned to do this in private, a public declaration would be more believable. It might be the only reason he got on that plane tomorrow. "We both knew what this was, Cody. It was never going to be anything. You were always leaving—"

"What if I stayed?"

"I don't want you to stay." Her raised voice turned the heads she needed. It took every ounce of willpower to pretend her heart wasn't shattering to do it. "I never wanted you to stay, don't you get that? This was only ever about the list."

Finally, Cody stood mute.

"Please come with me to the lawyer's office so we can be done with this prison sentence and both move on with our lives." She marched off, hardly able to keep up her icy façade. In the truck, she nearly broke down. But the tears would have to wait until she had those keys in hand. Once their task was legally complete, she could run and hide away in that cabin until he left Sunset Ridge. Maybe longer.

# CHAPTER SIXTEEN

CODY

Cody carried a steaming cup of coffee onto his covered beachfront lanai and settled in the uncomfortable lounge chair he swore he'd replace one of these days. He stared out at the water to distract himself from the aches and pains from the week of work. Maui sunrises were good for that sort of thing.

But no matter how much he tried to clear his head, too many thoughts loitered.

Two weeks in Maui should be enough to be in a solid groove of this next chapter. He always felt a little homesick during his time away, but never like this. A FaceTime call with Haylee and Melly made him physically ache for hours after it ended. Sadie still wasn't talking to him, but he heard about her perfect attendance at the store from Mom's daily email updates. Even Marc's short text messages made him wish he was there in person to call out his grumpiness.

Then there was Jenna Kingsley.

Distance should be all he needed to move on from that one whirlwind week. The ocean between them should've delivered clarity by now. Clarity on what in the world made him think he was in love with someone he hardly knew. Someone who clearly didn't feel the same way.

Except he still dreamed about her every night. He couldn't bring himself to delete the photos they no longer needed now that she'd gotten her cabin keys. Too often, he caught himself scrolling through and stopping on his favorites. Especially the one from the eagle sighting with the blurry bird. Her dazzling smile would be forever burned in his memory, even without the photo.

Too many times he'd nearly called her, but the unanswered texts he'd sent while in the Anchorage airport kept him from making a fool of himself.

A FaceTime call rang through on his phone, and he lit up at the sight of Melly's face on his screen. Talking to his family was truly the highlight of his time in Maui these two weeks. He'd skipped all the outings with the cast and crew of the show, and even turned down an offer to go kite surfing—the number-one thing on his Maui bucket list. All because he couldn't stand the thought of missing a single text.

"You look way too miserable for a beach bum

adrenaline junkie with an ocean view right off his back porch," Haylee said when he answered the call.

"Yeah, definitely." Sadie's face popped into the frame. "Why don't you trade me? I'll move to Maui and live your life, and you can come home. I'll even cut my hair and dye it blonde if that's what the part requires."

Cody was stunned to see the two side by side without one trying to strangle the other. Maybe this call on his beachfront porch was a dream. He looked down at his full coffee cup, questioning if it was real. It was his first cup, and he hadn't even touched it.

"You can't move to Maui now," Haylee said to Sadie. "Not after I helped you move all your crap home. I'm still sore from carrying that stupid dresser you couldn't live without."

"Okay, fair enough." Sadie returned her attention to the screen and waved her fingers at Cody. "I have to get to work. My boss says I can't take any vacation time until I can afford my own plane ticket to Maui."

Haylee watched something off-screen, returning her attention to Cody after a door closed. "Who would've thought she'd still be in Sunset Ridge? It's a miracle."

Though he wanted to ask what had brought the two sisters together, he didn't want to jinx it. Instead, he asked, "Where's my favorite niece?"

"Mom's giving her a bath." Loud rustling tore through the phone, and Cody pulled it away until

Haylee came back with a tortilla chip. "Are you happy, Cody?"

"Of course I am."

She crunched on the chip, taking her time to fire back a firm answer. "Liar."

"Why wouldn't I be happy?"

"Because you miss us. Like *really* miss us this time."

He couldn't deny she was right. Yesterday, he'd nearly broken his arm performing a dangerous stunt and it reminded him of something Jenna had said to him when they first met. One mistake could cost him his life. One slipup and he might never see his family or home again. Never before had that pesky thought troubled him. Now, he couldn't *stop* thinking about it. "Of course I miss you guys."

"Then come home."

"It's not that easy." It was, though. If he walked off set and headed straight to the airport, he'd forfeit three million dollars. The next guy in line would take his spot. And Cody would officially retire from being a stuntman to start the next chapter of his life. But the idea of being in Sunset Ridge knowing that Jenna never felt the same way about him was a hard pill to swallow. They'd run into each other. It was impossible not to in a small town.

"She loves you, you know."

"Who? Melly?"

"Well, duh. Of course Melly loves you." Haylee rolled her eyes as she propped her phone up to free her hands. She folded her arms on the counter and leaned forward, lowering her voice. "You know who I'm talking about. Jenna."

"You were there for the public embarrassment, right?" He scrubbed a hand over his face and sat back in his chair.

"She was lying."

"Don't think so."

Haylee let out a dramatic *ugh*. "Sometimes, you're too much of a guy, Cody. Seriously. Why do you think she did that?"

"Because she got what she wanted."

"You remember that rom-com you did a few years ago? The one where the girl lied because she thought she was doing the right thing? Jenna *loves* you."

Cody took a sip of coffee, but its bitter flavor made him abandon the cup. Yeah, he definitely wasn't feeling like himself right now. "My life isn't some movie, Haylee. Humiliating someone in front of half the town isn't the way real people declare their love."

"She had to make sure you believed her. So you would get on the plane."

"That doesn't make any—" In an instant, the truth rushed Cody like a tidal wave. Jenna told him about her older sister putting her life on hold to raise her, and always holding that over her head. No matter what Jenna did, it wasn't enough to appease Whitney. No, the older sister harbored resentment for the time she could never get back. It created an irreversible rift in their relationship.

How did he not understand that Jenna was protecting herself—and him—by turning back into the icy person he'd met when she first arrived? Of course she'd do it in front of witnesses. He'd broken through her toughest walls. If they'd been alone, she would've caved.

"Is it clicking into place *now?*" Haylee asked.

"Yeah." Cody popped up from his chair, overwhelmed by the dozens of things he'd have to do to get out of here. But the first one was all that mattered: booking that plane ticket home. He was leaving today. "Haylee—"

"Shut up and get packed. And don't you dare come home first. You go straight to Jenna's cabin and tell her how you feel or I'm not letting you see Melly."

"That's harsh."

"Love you!" Haylee ended the call, and Cody sprang into action packing a bag. He could send for the rest. He paid three months' rent when he moved in. The least the landlord could do with a place he was going to turn around and immediately re-rent was send Cody's things back to him in Alaska.

Back *home* where he belonged.

# CHAPTER SEVENTEEN

Jenna

Jenna held a framed drawing in her hands, tearing up at the unexpected find. She'd been in Grandpa's cabin two weeks now, but every day, a new treasure or secret surfaced. Her first day, she found an old photo album filled with her grandparents' traveling adventures. She'd spent hours savoring every photograph.

Four days ago, she found a handwritten ledger in a locked desk drawer upstairs that tracked transactions from an account Grandpa called *My Best Investments*— including monthly payments he sent to Whitney during the time Jenna was going to school. They were sizable. The kinds of payments that made up for a tenant who didn't pay rent. What the ledger was doing in Alaska, she couldn't fathom. But it reassured her of one thing: she made the right decision by leaving her old life and starting a new one.

Today, her cherished discovery was a framed drawing of Graham Cracker—the cat she'd drawn at four years old. "Buddy, this is who you're named after."

Graham shoved his head beneath her elbow, demanding pets. The forlorn look in his big doe eyes suggested he wasn't thrilled about being named after a cat. Or maybe it was the absence of his shotgun-stealing buddy that had him moping around the cabin today.

"I miss him too, Graham Cracker." She set the framed picture on the kitchen counter and crouched to hug the pup. Later, when she found the energy—the will—she'd clean up the dusty frame and hang her cherished drawing above her new writing desk. It warmed her heart to know Grandpa kept it all these years.

Jenna grabbed a treat out of Graham's special treat cupboard and tossed it to him. The pup caught it in midair and happily trotted to his new favorite spot in the mornings—a sunbathed rug beside the double glass doors to the deck.

They were settling in comfortably.

If only the sight of her phone didn't make her heart ache. The cell reception at the cabin was nonexistent, except when she was upstairs. That's when the string of texts Cody sent from the airport infiltrated her resolve to hide away and ignore him. If the texts weren't enough to cripple her in sadness, the photos she couldn't bring herself to delete surely were. It might help if she stopped looking at them.

The only thing besides Graham keeping her from completely falling apart was her new book series. Her agent and editor were both over the moon with her new concept and eagerly awaiting the first book.

She couldn't be certain if Grandpa had designed the upstairs as *his* writing studio or hers. The unusual amount of painting and drawing supplies suggested he at least had her in mind when he set it up. Which begged the question that had continually nagged at her for months. How long had he known he was sick? He only told Jenna a few days before he passed that he wasn't going to make it through the summer. Made her promise that she'd make the trip to Alaska before the snow flew.

Now a three-inch layer of snow covered the ground surrounding the remote cabin. *Did he think he had more time?* No matter how much she searched through the cabin, she couldn't find any letter that might give her the answers she sought.

She left Graham basking in the sun in the dining area off the kitchen and sought out the cushy recliner in the living room. She'd taken many naps in it since she moved in. One sounded pretty darn good right about now.

She curled up with her favorite blanket and hugged it to her chest. What she wouldn't give to have Grandpa here with her now. She craved his wisdom about love, and desperately wanted to know if she'd made the right choice. She looked up at the vaulted cedar ceiling. "Anything? A sign? A ghostly laugh? Something to tell me if I made the *right* sacrifice for love. Or did I screw it all up?"

Graham let out a series of barks that catapulted her out of her chair. This far out, she was certain she'd encounter a bear sooner or later. She'd asked locals if they were hibernating yet, but the answers she got were mixed.

Jenna slipped into her fuzzy slippers and grabbed a baseball bat she found on her third day in the cabin. A bear would probably laugh at her if she swung it, but she hoped she could use it to intimidate one and scare it away. It could also be an intruder, in which case a bat might come in quite handy.

"Stay here, Graham." She pushed the door open enough to poke her head out through it, but whatever the disturbance was, it was coming from around the back. Quietly, she closed the door behind her and tiptoed over the snow she hadn't felt like shoveling off her deck.

When she rounded the corner, she screamed.

An enormous moose stood half on her deck, half off, snorting and scraping one hoof. Ed's attention was laser-focused on the man he'd cornered.

"Cody?"

"Surprise," he said with a weak laugh.

"Ed, what are you doing?" It was probably a bad idea to address the moose when he was clearly upset.

She'd never seen a moose charge someone, but if Ed could figure out how to get the rest of his heavy frame up those narrow stairs, she might have a new Alaskan experience to add to her list. "Ed, leave Cody alone."

"In his defense, he did chase me onto the deck instead of back to the water."

Jenna glanced toward the shore, surprised to see a bright blue kayak tied to a tree. "You do know there's a road here, right?"

"It's not plowed. My car got stuck half a mile in."

Never mind that seeing Cody here in Sunset Ridge, on *her* deck, should be impossible. Butterflies she thought had died came immediately back to life as she realized what lengths he'd gone to in order to see her. "Aren't you supposed to be in Maui?"

"Yes. No. Not anymore." Cody flattened his back against the cabin when Ed leapt forward. It was the reminder to them both that Ed wasn't some tame pet. He was a wild animal capable of serious damage.

"Hold on. I'll be right back," she called to Cody, running back into the house.

"Jenna—"

She zipped through the cabin, sprinting for the master bedroom that faced the bay. She shoved the window open, pushed out the screen, and yanked Cody inside. They fell back onto the bed with a bouncy plop. But before Jenna could take a single breath of relief, Ed stuck his snout through the opening and snorted.

Jenna curled into Cody, fearing Ed would knock down the logs with his antlers when he charged, wondering if Cody's embrace would be the last thing she remembered before her time on this world ended.

Graham charged into the room, barking at Ed like he was chewing the moose out. Ed's ears went down, then back up. He tilted his head in that odd way that only *this* moose could pull off. He turned his attention back to Jenna and Cody, who were wrapped up tight together. He straightened his crooked head and — "Did he just nod at us?" Jenna asked Cody, because it seemed too weird to be true.

"Okay, Ed. I believe in you," Cody said to the moose with a laugh. "Happy now?"

Ed retreated from the window. They lifted from the bed to the window in time to catch the moose trotting toward the woods. "Looks like you need some new deck steps," Cody mused.

Graham leapt onto the bed and smothered Cody with excited licks. The eager pup tackled him to the bed. The sound of Cody's laughter filled the empty holes in her heart. But before she dared to feel an ounce of hope, she had to get to the bottom of this. "Cody, why are you back?"

"I'm not just back," he said, forced to lift Graham in order to stand. "I'm *home*."

"But Maui—"

"Isn't what I want anymore."

"You gave up three million dollars?"

"It's only money." He set Graham onto the bed and reached for Jenna's hand. "I know why you lied, Jenna. I know what you were trying to do. But I went to Maui. I spent two weeks there trying to convince myself I was happy to be back on set, doing what I loved. But the truth was, I missed everything about Sunset Ridge. My family, my pitiful car, my favorite foods, my favorite four-legged buddy. But most of all, I missed the woman I'm *still* in love with."

"Cody—"

"I know it's crazy, Jenna. Who falls in love with someone they just met?"

"Grandpa Eddie did." Jenna reached for his cheek, tilting his head down to capture his attention. "It's not crazy, Cody. Because in that same week, I fell in love with you, too. I just couldn't stand the thought of you staying for me and resenting me for it later."

"Leaving is what proved to me that there is nowhere else I'd rather be."

"Even if I can't get over my fear of flying to travel anywhere else?"

"We're going to work on that."

"Cody, I'm not—" He silenced her with a kiss. The sudden brush of his lips took her by surprise, instantly making her knees weaker. She scooped a hand around his neck and held on for dear life as he deepened the kiss she was experiencing on a soul-deep level. It felt like jumping off a cliff and soaring through the air just realizing you can fly.

They were both breathless when they finally came

up for air. Graham paced on the bed behind Cody, desperate for his attention. Cody wrapped his arms around the pup in a big bear hug and squeezed. "You want a kiss too, buddy?"

"Does your family know you're back?"

"No. Thought we could tell them together."

Jenna narrowed her eyes at him. "You need someone to pull your car out of a snowbank."

Cody cupped her cheek, caressing her skin with his thumb. "And I don't feel like kayaking back to town. It's cold out there!"

Her gaze dropped to his lips once more, her body already tingling in anticipation of another toe-curling kiss. "Have you figured out what you're going to do all winter?"

"Besides loving on you?"

Jenna rolled her eyes at him playfully, secretly thrilled by his response.

"I have all winter to figure it out. Maybe I'll try writing a book." He drew her in for another kiss that caused Graham to groan and drop onto the bed with a dramatic thud. Her heart was filled to the brim with love.

# EPILOGUE

Sadie

Sadie Evans stepped out of the bush plane and onto the rocky shore near Bear Glacier. A chilly spring breeze cut through her lightweight sweater, but she wasn't going to curse Cody and Jenna for picking this remote spot exposed to glacial gusts of wind for their wedding. Oh, no. She was becoming a better person. Better people didn't complain about trivial things.

"What a beautiful day for a wedding. Sun's shining, skies are clear, the water's pristine," Mom gushed as she came up beside Sadie, tears pricking the corners of her eyes. There hadn't been a wedding among the Evans clan since Laurel and Chase married almost six years ago, despite Mom's not-so-subtle hints that the recently reunited couple have a vow renewal. She loved an excuse to throw a party.

"That mascara isn't waterproof," Sadie warned lightheartedly. "At least wait until *after* pictures to cry."

"I'm just so happy." She tucked herself into the crook of Dad's arm when he made it around the side of the plane, and he kissed the top of her head. Sadie felt her heart swell with hope that someday she'd find the same kind of love her parents had. Not that she would openly admit that since she was on a dating hiatus for the foreseeable future, advice courtesy of Cody's tough love.

Between all the drama with Aaron that led to an explosive, final breakup and embarrassingly throwing herself at her former boss at an office party for the whole company to witness, Sadie needed to steer clear of men until she got her own head on straight. She wasn't foolish enough to believe a measly seven months was long enough to fix everything inside her that was broken.

The three stepped a safe distance from the plane, allowing Liam to take off to pick up the next round of Evanses. The bride-to-be would be dropped off last.

She spotted Cody on the shore, arms folded over his chest, deep in conversation with Marc. The photographer stood off to the side, snapping pictures. She was the only non-family member allowed at the small, private ceremony.

Since Cody made the decision to call Sunset Ridge home permanently, his relationship with Marc

had vastly improved. So much so that Marc was offi-
ciating the wedding today. If Sadie was being honest,
she was jealous at how effortlessly things amended
between them. If it killed her, she'd prove to Marc
that she was responsible, trustworthy, and most
importantly, mature.

"I'm going to go talk to Cody," she told Mom and
Dad. She twisted her curled hair into a ponytail and
held on as she crossed the white rock beach, stepping
over stray branches as she went. There wasn't enough
hairspray in the world to protect her efforts from
glacial winds.

But this was Sadie's chance to right a wrong that'd
haunted her for months. It was now or never.

"That's great news," she heard Cody say to Marc.
"I had no idea how you were going to run the clinic
by yourself." Sadie suspected they were talking about
the vet clinic. Marc's partner was retiring next
month, leaving Marc as the sole veterinarian in town.
He already worked long hours and most weekends as
it was. Alone, he'd be completely swamped. Her
eldest brother never turned away an animal he
thought he could help.

"Great news?" Sadie repeated, using her sweetest
smile.

Marc frowned, but she didn't take it personally
since it was his go-to expression in most situations.

"Is it top secret?" Sadie teased, refusing to accept
defeat. She'd already made tremendous progress with
Haylee and Laurel these past few months. Sticking

around for more than a couple of weeks at a time had its benefits. That and keeping her mouth shut instead of snapping defensively at every jab. If she could retrain herself to think before she spoke, she could and *would* break through Marc's walls one of these days.

"I found another partner to take Doc Baker's place," Marc finally answered.

"His buddy from vet school," Cody added. "Conner Michaelson, did you say?'

Marc nodded.

"Wow, that's great news," Sadie agreed. It took some effort, but she set aside her own needs to talk to focus on how this would benefit Marc. She was a work in progress, but at least she was headed in the right direction. "You found someone who's willing to uproot everything and move to Alaska?"

"I did."

"His family's okay with relocating to a remote small town in the middle of nowhere?" Polite conversation to express interest? *Check*.

"Don't," Marc said so firmly is caught Sadie off guard.

"Don't what?"

"Don't go fishing for information." Marc let out a heavy sigh that was closer to a groan. Shoving his hands in his front slacks pockets, he added, "Conner's a good man. Just leave him be, okay? It's a miracle he's coming at all, and the last thing I need is you ruining it."

Sadie forced herself to swallow hard—twice—and *still* needed to bite her tongue. She wasn't *fishing* for information about this Conner's marital status for her own sake. Polite conversation managed? *Uncheck.*

If Cody hadn't been standing right there, reminding her with his very presence that repairing her relationship with Marc would take time, she would've slipped up for sure. Ran that troublesome mouth of hers and only made things worse. She wanted to say something—anything that would make the situation not so tense—but instead, she turned to Cody. "Can I talk to you for a minute? Please?"

Cody nodded.

Marc turned abruptly and marched off toward their parents.

"I'm proud of you," Cody said.

"That wasn't easy," Sadie muttered as the distant roar of an engine echoed in the sky. "But that's not what I need to talk to you about."

"What is it?"

"I need to apologize."

Cody's eyebrows drew in confusion. "For what?"

Sadie sucked in a deep breath and let it out even slower. Her words, however, came out in a quick jumble. "I'm the one who told Jenna to let you go to Maui. I'm the reason she told you she didn't want you to stay. I have a feeling you already know that, but I needed to tell you. I needed you to hear it from me. I'm sorry, Cody. I never should've interfered. I was worried you'd stay here and resent the decision later—"

"Hey," Cody said, placing both hands on her shoulders, waiting until she looked up at him. "I forgive you."

Sadie looked at him suspiciously. "Just like that?"

"You're right, I already knew. But I'm glad you told me. It took courage, Sadie."

Maybe it was a sign of maturity that she felt she was getting let off the hook too easily. "But I could've ruined everything."

"But you didn't." Cody glanced at the plane touching down, watching with Sadie as Chase, Laurel, and their newly adopted son, Eli, stepped out of the plane. Sadie's heart warmed again at the sight. Seven-year-old Eli fit perfectly into their clan from day one. He'd stolen all their hearts with his zest for adventure, infectious smile, and never-ending thirst for knowledge. For the first time in her twenty-six years, Sadie considered having kids of her own someday.

"You really forgive me?" Sadie asked Cody as Liam took off again to pick up the last round of passengers, which would include Cody's bride-to-be. "You're not just saying that so I'll stop being a pest on your wedding day?"

"I chose to come back because I was miserable away from *all* of you. Not just Jenna."

"But most importantly Jenna."

"Yes," he said with an easy laugh that allowed some of her tension to dissipate. "I was running from my feelings. I was the only one who could bring myself back to face them."

For years, Cody showed absolutely no interest in ever settling down. Let alone getting married. But the way he looked at Jenna . . . "Do you think I'll ever find someone who's actually good for me?" Sadie asked honestly.

"Yes, I do."

"You sound so sure of yourself."

"Because I am."

"But how?" Sadie had a proven track record of bad relationship decisions. She seemed to be hopelessly drawn to the wrong sort of man and paid dearly for it with each crushing heartbreak. Yet she still longed for someone who would sweep her off her feet and make her forget about all those mistakes. Cody was the only person she'd been honest with about that.

"Stop looking for him," Cody said, using that all-too-familiar nonchalant tone that drove her mad.

Sadie frowned at him. "You make it sound so simple."

"It *is* simple. We're the ones who overcomplicate it."

The crunch of rocks warned Sadie their moment alone was nearly over. A quick turn of her head over her shoulder confirmed it. The Evans clan, minus Haylee and Melly who would be on that last flight, were descending on the ceremony spot with the glacier view. "But—"

"We need to get into place, everyone," Mom announced, using that familiar authority in her tone that snapped everyone to attention.

As they obeyed and moved to their designated places, Sadie heard the distant roar of the plane engine again. Her concerns about life and love would have to wait. It wasn't as if she didn't have time. Well, unless Dad really *did* sell the store. Then she'd need to find a new job. The thought made her heart squeeze with sadness. It was strange to be remiss about the store changing ownership when she'd never cared about it before. *Maybe I can convince Dad to change his—*

Laurel elbowed Sadie, shaking her from her thoughts as the plane touched down. "Smile," her older sister instructed. "Today is all about Cody and Jenna, remember?"

"Right." For the first time, Sadie didn't have to bite down on a snappy retort to such a comment. She smiled. Maybe there was hope for her after all.

She watched with the rest of the clan as Jenna stepped out of the plane in an elegantly simple white gown with a band of white flowers in her hair. She'd been smarter to style it up so the wind couldn't destroy her curls. Even from a distance, Jenna looked positively radiant.

"I thought she didn't like to fly," Sadie whispered to Laurel.

"Cody's been taking her out once a week since he decided to stay," Laurel answered as Haylee emerged from the opposite side of the plane, holding Melly on a hip with one arm and guiding Graham on a leash with the other. The pup let out a few enthusiastic barks, announcing the bride. "Graham, too. They fly better together."

Sadie looked back at her brother, the emotion etched on his face hitting her square in the chest. She wiped away a tear pricking the corner of her eye. Okay, now she understood why Mom was a blubbering, happy mess. With the stunning Alaska landscape and view of Bear Glacier, the small gathering of family, and the abundance of happiness and love emitting from each and every one of them, this moment felt like a fairytale.

Sadie vowed that one day she would find a man who looked at her the same way Cody was looking at Jenna walking down the aisle.

Sign up for Jacqueline Winter's newsletter to receive alerts about current projects and new releases!

http://eepurl.com/du18iz

# OTHER BOOKS BY JACQUELINE WINTERS

SWEET ROMANCE

Sunset Ridge Series
    1 - Moose Be Love
    2 - My Favorite Moosetake
    3 - Annoymoosely Yours
    4 - Love & Moosechief
    5 - Under the Mooseltoe
    6 - Moosely Over You
    7 - Absomoosely in Love
    8 - Perfectly Moosematched

Starlight Cowboys Series
    1 - Cowboys & Starlight
    2 - Cowboys & Firelight
    3 - Cowboys & Sunrises
    4 - Cowboys & Moonlight
    5 - Cowboys & Mistletoe

6 - Cowboys & Shooting Stars

Christmas in Snowy Falls
    1 - Pawsitively in Love Again at Christmas
    2 - Pawsitively Home for Christmas
    3 - Pawsitively Yours for Christmas

Stand-Alone
    *Hooked on You

---

## STEAMY ROMANTIC SUSPENSE

Willow Creek Series
    1 - Sweetly Scandalous
    2 - Secretly Scandalous
    3 - Simply Scandalous

# ABOUT THE AUTHOR

Jacqueline Winters has been writing since she was nine when she'd sneak stacks of paper from her grandma's closet and fill them with adventure. She grew up in small-town Nebraska and spent a decade living in beautiful Alaska. She writes sweet contemporary romance and contemporary romantic suspense.

She's a sucker for happily ever after's, has a sweet tooth that can be sated with cupcakes. On a relaxing evening, you can find her at her computer writing her next novel with her faithful dog poking his adorable nose over her keyboard.

Made in the USA
Coppell, TX
04 March 2022

74408876R00132